LAURE-ANNE TOUJOURS

'Tell me, Sylvain,' said my husband, 'what do you think of Laure-Anne? She knows how to pick a dress and she can vary the *décolleté*. Show them, my dear, let the gentlemen see your assets.'

'Really, Serge,' I protested.

'Come, *mon trésor*, we're all friends here. Show them your tits.'

The whole table was laughing except me. Georges gingerly pulled on my left sleeve whereupon Sylvain pulled on the other side. I made a grab for their wrists but it was useless. They pulled the top of my dress down past the point of no return and my breasts suddenly spilled out.

'Lovely!' cried Claire. 'What a fabulous bosom!'

LAURE-ANNE TOUJOURS

The continuing story of Laure-Anne D. as told
to Nicholas Courtin

NEXUS

A Nexus Book
published by
the Paperback Division of
W.H. Allen & Co Plc

A Nexus Book
Published in 1990
by the Paperback Division of
W H Allen & Co plc
Sekforde House, 175/9 St John Street
London EC1V 4LL

Printed and bound in Great Britain by
Cox & Wyman Ltd, Reading
ISBN 0 352 32642 5

Chapter One

It was the Englishman's lustful appraisal of my body in the foyer of our honeymoon hotel that finally made me realise that I was now a married woman and no longer free to play the field.

The elderly gentleman's pudgy nose and ginger moustache appeared over the edge of the *Daily Telegraph* as he surveyed me from the safety of his big armchair. Nobody had told me he was looking at me, of course, but women know when they are being inspected, and they can no more avoid sneaking a backward glance at an admirer than they can ignore a mirror. The stranger's glance, which lasted no more than half a second, was sufficient to tell me that he had already studied every centimetre of me as I stood at the reception desk. I could almost hear the urgent messages rushing to the eros centre in his brain. But if he obeyed the signals he was doomed to failure, for Serge alone had the right to touch me now.

Turning to face my husband, I drew a deep breath. At that moment, no medieval maiden about to submit to her lord's *droit de seigneur* could have been more apprehensive than I. I was certain that our wedding night would be rapturous, surpassing anything I had ever experienced before. And so it turned out. Which is why I want to record it in detail, in view of what followed.

We had abstained from love-making, for six weeks, actually 39 days and 38 nights. In that period we were so chaste that sometimes I feared Serge would call it all off. He was distant and irritable all the time, so much so that more than once I wondered whether we were asking too much of ourselves. By the time we came to check into Pooley's Hotel in London to begin our honeymoon we were as randy as a pair of rabbits – although we were careful not to offend British decorum by showing it.

'Bonjour,' Inspector Serge Brossard said to the desk clerk, forgetting that French is not quite the universal language it would like to be. I risked another glance at the man with the newspaper; he was still staring at me and I stuck my nose in the air, shaking out my ash-blond curls. My husband saw the exchange and with a twitch of the head ordered me to stand closer to him.

Everything had gone off well: the girls from the club escorting me to Avallon town hall in carloads, all dressed to kill; Serge's colleagues greeting us with their tongues hanging out as they gave me the once-over. Then came the brief ceremony and a buffet that was almost as hurried because everyone had to get away. Afterwards, Serge and I made a three-hour dash northwards to Roissy Airport, and took off for London. Where it was raining and chilly and we even rejoiced at that because it seemed so appropriate for a March afternoon provided by Her Britannic Majesty. I had been the one to pick London. In the taxi from the airport I had been enthralled. It was my first visit and I had babbled away entranced at everything: the buses of course, the advertisement hoardings, driving on the left, the great shops like Harrods and Fortnum and Mason. I ignored every detail that was much the same as elsewhere in Europe and saw differences where none existed, for example the hotel awning and the man with the big umbrella who saw us across the pavement.

I felt that I had now reached safe harbour and won my man, and I had a platinum wedding ring to prove it. I would now set up home with my husband and have lots of new friends and babies and make them all happy. I was a radiant 29 and I felt heady and triumphant. I remember so many small details. At the desk a porter waited with our luggage, while a lad helped me off with my blue-grey coat edged with chinchilla. I wanted to show off my outfit, a russet low-waisted cotton dress by Louis Féraud, with tiny pleats in the flared skirt. I fiddled with the sapphire engagement ring next to my platinum ring, and with Serge's present on my right wrist, a four-strand pearl bracelet with a silver clasp, which he claimed he had 'got cheap' outside a Nice casino!

'My nem ees Brossard, we 'ave a room reservated, I sink,' declared my spouse. I gave his arm a squeeze and looked round slyly to see who else was watching us. We were the centre of attention, and I hurriedly turned round; there was no need to show everyone that I was about to change at any moment from a refined young lady into a raving nymphomaniac in the arms of my husband. I was clenching my thighs together so tightly they hurt.

A uniformed girl of my own age glided up the counter and marked something in a book; our eyes met and we exchanged a friendly smile. The lazy tick of a grandfather clock caught my attention, the time-piece stood at the foot of the stairs next to a large tub of greenery. The reassuring smells of the old hotel – leather, cigar smoke, discreet perfume – helped to calm me down.

'Will you be dining at the hotel this evening?' the desk clerk enquired.

I moved forward: 'When is the latest we can have a light meal and a drink?' My vocabulary was just a little better than Serge's.

'You may have a drink any time, but we do not like to take orders for dinner after 11, madam.' I liked the clipped *madam* in preference to our *madame*, as it summed up everything I thought I knew about the English.

'Then we'll have it just before 11.'

'That will be fine, Mrs Brossard.' The *Mrs* was amusing, but it didn't feel like me.

Then we were moving to the lift, and I was beaming so royally that my jaw muscles ached.

Now we were inside the lemon-hued room and the porter was backing out with his tip. I just had time to note the quality of the cheerful modern paintings before, like all newly-weds, we sank into an endless embrace. 'Happy?' Serge murmured, and I blessed him for being so unoriginal and for avoiding some silly wisecrack. He added: 'It's been a tough month. I'm glad it's raining, rain stirs my sap.'

'Mine too. Keep yours simmering while I take a shower. But first you may undress the bride.' This he proceeded to do, exclaiming at the absence of any knickers, and I told him: 'They were auctioned at the restaurant, remember? All my others are packed.'

'You mean we've come all this way without panties?'

'I have, I don't know about you,' I remarked, skipping into the bathroom.

'If I'd known I'd have tried something on the plane.'

'And spoilt my dress,' I shouted above the woosh of the shower. 'In any case you did try, and that was enough to remind me I had a body.' I soaped myself. 'Tell me, *mon amour*, you have really waited for me? You haven't been doing things on your own?'

'Hah, whoever heard of a cop who wanks!'

'True, they don't spread it around much in the media.'

'How about you?'

'I swear I didn't,' I yelled back. 'But I kept remembering, I had sleepless nights thinking about us fucking on the plaid blanket in front of your electric fire.'

'We'll have a real log fire in the new place.'

I sauntered out in my embroidered blue silk wrap, which he was seeing for the first time: 'If I'd known six weeks would last so long, we'd have done it more that evening.'

'I wanted to.' We hugged for a long while, then he undid the belt of the wrap. Serge was already unclothed, save for his yellow briefs that showed off his half-erect cock. I had chosen them for him, as I liked the way they highlighted this particular policeman's truncheon. Tilting my head I said: 'Take them off, they clash with the wallpaper. You know, I don't think you look like J. F. Kennedy after all, more like Yves Montand in his prime.'

4

'Never seen him in yellow underpants. Why can't I just be good old Serge Brossard, *Inspecteur SRPJ?*'

'I've no objection. But one day I'm going to undress on my own and make you keep all your clothes on. I love being kissed by fully-dressed cops.'

'Just make sure this one's the last in the series.'

'Curiously enough, you're the first in that category.'

A sigh escaped me as his fat bulge pressed into my abdomen. He made no effort to remove his pants – the bastard was obviously going to tease me to my first orgasm. I hoisted myself on tiptoe so that his cock and balls were squashed against my mound and my arms snaked round his neck. I wriggled against him and his chest hairs tickled my breasts. 'It's you from now on, but if you start anything with another woman I'll shoot your nuts off with that MAC 50 of yours. Have you brought it with you?'

'Not allowed. Anyhow it's a new model now, a . . .'

I placed a finger on his lips, he fondled my neck and I played with his thick wavy black hair: 'Your gun, the one I'm really interested in, is my property now. I bought it with my savings.' The wrap slipped to the floor.

My last remark referred to the sale of Les Chabannes, the private sex club I had set up with friends after the years at the Top Club in Paris as a hostess. Les Chabannes, a remote old farmhouse near Avallon, had been operating for about a year when we agreed I should sell up my 51% stake, a quick decision approved by my accountant who conceded that the profits were starting to justify a snap sale. The money was due to be paid into our joint account any day now.

Serge was becoming rock hard. His hands slid down to fondle my bottom. I leant back to admire him, but I kept my crotch glued to his stiff organ.

'Yours is the most perfect body in the world,' he stated. 'But it would be a mere work of art without those lovely candid eyes and the fascinating gap in your top teeth.'

Suddenly he let go of me and produced the Armagnac we had already opened on the plane. Perhaps the poor fellow was a little nervous and needed to build up his courage. Well, if he wanted to keep his pants on it was all right by me, we had a lifetime ahead of us. We each took a swig, and he put the bottle on the dresser, clearing his throat: 'Yes, you've paid for me. You know, when I was at the *lycée* a whole gang of us used to pay girls for pictures.'

'Pictures!'

'We would get them into one of those photo cubicles at Chatelet Metro station and they posed for us kneeling on the stool with their skirts up. Five francs a photo.'

'Dirty little puppies,' I whispered. 'There's no charge for anything tonight.'

Then his pants were off and all the lights were out except one by the bed. I lay back on the sheets as Serge passionately kissed my thighs, slowly working upwards from my knees to my crotch and back again. Time and again he stopped short of my fleece, and then suddenly his snout was deep in my wet pussy, rooting at me like a pig after truffles. As the long-awaited sensation flooded through me I closed my eyes in abandon. An age went by and I came twice before he moved away and I opened my eyes to see his erupting prick big and bold in his hand and a look of anguish on his countenance. My lover gulped in air and his crisis subsided, and I loved him for reaching a peak so quickly. I held out my arms to him and his still-erect tool was at my entrance, arousing me with little jabs. I guided him impatiently into my sacred folds and, as he penetrated me, he kissed me soulfully. Then he flung his head back and uttered a wail, his face contorted in passion. A firm thrust, and he lost control, ransacking my body, bumping into me with such force that my frame juddered and my pelvis humped rhythmically. Our lips joined greedily and his tongue bullied its way into my mouth. I wrenched my head clear and as we climaxed my teeth sank into his shoulder and he twined his fingers in my hair. '*Nom d'un chien!*' he cried out. We bit and clawed and spat, all thought suspended, yielding to our lust in a sweat-drenched paroxysm of joy.

We were speechless for a full minute. Then I said: 'That, *chéri*, felt like original sin. Now I can understand it!'

'We've waited so long, it was like the first time all over again!'

I rolled my head contentedly on the pillow: 'You've never been so superb. You've no idea how intoxicating it is to be desired like that, to be taken and dominated, to . . .'

He clamped a hand over my mouth, and switched on the radio by the bed.

'We need another drink,' he growled, staggering across the room for the Armagnac and lighting a cigarette.

But I remained in another world: 'I drank you with my whole body, it was like drowning in a sea of sensation. I never imagined it was possible to feel such pleasure . . .'

My mouth was wide open when the neck of the bottle was thrust between my lips. I sat up choking and spluttering, tears of laughter and fury blinding me, as Serge licked the spilled liquid from my breasts.

'I love you deeply, Serge. *Je t'aime-je t'aime-je t'aime.*'

'I'll adore you for ever, Laure-Anne my princess.'

I grinned back: 'You more or less implied it at the town hall, but I shall need more proof tonight.'

I wanted to make love again at once, and took a begonia from the enormous vase of flowers on the table by the window. I began to stroke him with the begonia – all over his chest, and thighs and genitals.

'Oh look,' I cried out, 'the wardrobe's got mirrors all over it. Let's make love in front of it, I've always wanted to do that. Stand up and I'll give you a blow-job and we can watch ourselves. My word, you're getting it up already. Did you know that 130 millilitres of extra blood is surging into your cock right now? I read about it.'

'How do they know? Sounds frightening.'

I stood him sideways to the mirror with his hands on his hips and we put another light on. On my knees, I caressed his penis and scrotum with the flower and then with my fingers and my hair. No man can resist a kneeling woman and Serge's glistening prick stood straight and thick, the glans now a bulbous purple heart as I slid back the foreskin. His bag hung full and round and luscious. 'It's beautiful, *mon chou*, it really is,' I pronounced, whereupon he glowed with pride. 'You realise,' I continued, 'that this is the first time I have had your thing to myself for ages. I'll make you keep coming, all night, and each time you'll like it better. I warn you I'm insatiable.'

My fluttering tongue tormented the tiny hole at the end of his tool, and, as I teased it, he gently pulled the hair on the back of my neck. This hunk of man was completely in my power now as my lips slowly encompassed the heavy shaft, going down on it as far as I could, then pulling back and sucking hard. I kept going for minute upon minute, glancing repeatedly at the mirror to see Serge's eyes glued to the image of my bottom as it ballooned and contracted with my movements. To enhance the pleasure I fondled myself between my legs. 'Oh yes,' he rasped, reaching down to cup my dangling breasts.

'Quick,' I ordered. 'Sit on the bed.' He was in position like a shot and, with my back to him, I sat on his lap with my legs apart so that his penis stood erect along my crack. Slowly I closed my legs to feel his stiff weapon while he slapped my boobies making them wobble, then I spread myself open again and repeated the movement. The sight of my lewd actions, along with the spectacle of his balls rising and falling in time with his great cock, was one of the most erotic visions I had ever experienced. I knew that Serge felt the same way. 'I'm almost there,' he breathed hotly into my neck. I put my hands behind me to seize his waist, his fingers tightened on my tits and we froze just in time to watch his sperm pump out creamily and fall onto the carpet.

My partner moaned and collapsed backward onto the bed and, after a moment in which to recover, I set about cleaning the carpet. After all, one has one's standards of decency.

Rejoining him on the bed, I whispered, 'Wasn't that something!'

'*Nom d'un chien*, it felt like molten steel, I nearly passed out.'

I bathed him in cool water like a big baby, and took a

long shower myself, returning to find him already quite perky anew. He said, 'You're one down on me, lie back and read something, this for example.' And he threw a travel brochure at me.

It was about Guernsey and I said: 'Where's Guernsey?'

'Off the west coast of Scotland.'

'Hm. Funny place to grow tomatoes.' I read aloud as he licked my feet and I added: 'They speak Norman patois, I don't think it's off Scotland at all. Did we invade Scotland?'

'Sure thing. Captured a bloke called Charlie. Keep reading.'

I recited: '*The islanders are fond of reminding visitors that England is a possession of theirs, and has been since 1066* – Is that what they call British humour?'

'Lift your legs higher.'

'Yes Serge. *The title of Duke of Normandy has remained to this day and Guernsey's loyal toast is "The Queen, our duke"* – That's ridiculous, must be a misprint.'

'Don't be too sure. Stop rocking.'

'I can't stop, you're driving me frantic. I'm fed up with reading, can't we put the light out? Then I can really let myself go.'

'We'll keep the light on. I want to see you open up like a flower. Put this pillow under you.'

'Yes, Serge. *Perhaps part of Parliament's success is due to there being no political parties or any opposition.* That makes sense. Aarrh, that's good, mmmm. You're biting, it's no good I can't go on, ayeeee . . .'

His lips were tugging at my clitoris, his nose easing my vaginal lips apart, his mouth enclosing my entire entrance. I read a few more words, but rippling waves of pleasure were turning me into a frenzied animal. Serge was blowing on me and lapping me, tickling my back entrance at every lick. I squawked on: '*The beaches have no promenades or piers and you will find no roundabouts or candy floss . . .*

'Please Serge, I feel utterly debauched but I can't come like this.'

Serge's right hand was pumping away at his prick, and the sight of this suddenly triggered in me an unstoppable flood of lascivious pleasure. I gripped my love's head between my thighs and bucked and bucked in a long orgasm.

He was furious, muttering '*putain de putain*' as I released him. He could hardly have summed it up better.

We dozed off, but at 10.30 p.m. Serge opened a window and told me to ring down for refreshment. This involved a complicated three-sided bilingual parley, after which we put the room to rights and made ourselves look respectable. I made the matrimonial bed look rather less like a François Boucher painting, but the almond fragrance of sperm was still quite pungent.

We finally went to sleep properly around midnight, and the next thing I knew my husband was again forcing my legs apart and climbing on top of me.

'*Mon amour*,' I mumbled, precisely as the great man's rod jabbed at my fragile pussy with the urgency of a fencer's epée. 'Ow!' I protested.

'I want another poke,' he snapped, thrusting into my sleepy quim.

'Eeee!' I jumped.

'I want you tight like a virgin.'

I fought him but he had my arms pinned. A mighty heave, and he penetrated me without mercy. Bone-hard flesh ripped into me and I was terrified. But my expression must have excited him, for he gathered my breasts in his big palms and mauled them cruelly. I shrieked out, where-upon he stuck a pillow over my face and I thrashed about in a frantic attempt to escape suffocation. My head emerged, for his grip had shifted down my body and his hands were ravaging my buttocks. He lifted me up half dead, and I was as responsive as a doll when he jerked out his climax.

A minute later my assailant apologised. 'I'm sorry, *chérie*, it's those extra millilitres of blood, I couldn't resist you, you looked so pure. I've always wanted to take a girl who's entirely defenseless. Forgive me, I'll never . . .'

'Forgive you! I'm sure you've torn something, it feels like barbed wire in there. What's the time?'

'Six in the morning.'

During those first 36 hours, the bridegroom had me length-wise, crosswise and half under the bed. I rode on him as he sat on a chair, clung to him as he stood with my legs wrapped round his middle, kept him hard inside me for a whole 30 minutes while I forced him to wait, offered myself on all fours and bent myself double with my legs round his neck. We also broke new ground for both of us in the lotus position. He tried to sodomise me, but I refused outright, threatening to call the management.

By the second breakfast we were sore and exhausted, Serge's prick was as red as a carrot and my vagina so sensitive I had to douche myself with cool water time and again for relief.

Subsequently we hired a small car and drove to the Here-ford area where we booked into a country pub and slept for 14 hours without a break. Serge woke with a giant erection and had to march round the room until it went flaccid and he could use the bathroom, a sight that set me off in a fit of giggling. We toured England and Scotland and terminated our honeymoon at Pooley's for one last night before flying home.

Yes, I was proud to be a married woman, was looking forward to a settled life after years of toil as a mercenary in the sex service industry. I was looking forward to a conventionally happy future.

When you have enjoyed money and the power to do anything you want, and have done it, there is nothing left but drugs, death or normality. I chose normality, and no one seemed more normal than my husband.

I had met Serge when the extortion mob moved in on us at Les Chabannes. I had refused to play ball and, to cut the story short, was held for ransom for a brief time near Lyon. Inspector Brossard, who had been keeping an eye on the club, led the team who rescued me. Thus he became my hero – anyway I had been trying to hook him for weeks!

I had had enough of promiscuous sex, and the AIDS scare blew up about then. Though not actually adhering to the New Chastity movement I was running scared. Serge was my lucky break, my chance to quit the sex business. I grabbed it with both hands. I flung myself at him, and in the confusion it was difficult to gauge the precise nature of his love for me, or its depth. Which is really what this book is all about. What mattered to me when we reached London was that I worshipped *him*, from his raven hair and clear grey eyes to the toes of his off duty policeman's shoes. This steady, reliable and honest man had taken me in, so to speak, and in return I would make his happiness my prime concern. Our romantic *voyage de noces* had done nothing to indicate that I was making a mistake.

Even so, the rape-of-the-virgin-bride scene was hard to accept. Another thing: he repeatedly called me his 'baby doll' in English on the flight back to Roissy. I smiled feebly but kept my own counsel, disliking the image. If that was how he saw me we would have some talking to do and I would gradually steer him away from the concept.

In any case, as everyone knows, French wives always make their point in the end. Or so they say.

Chapter Two

After a month-long interlude with Les Brossards camped in Serge's sparsely furnished police flat, we moved into an apartment in la rue du Chateau, which we did out in a mixture of period and modern. It was in an old 1930's building that had been renovated to provide a large living room while sacrificing the second bedroom. In this living room we installed a new fireplace. Luckily we were able to occupy the place quickly as the vendor was decent, we were paying cash and a police officer buyer is as safe as the Banque de France.

In that Spring of 1985 I did not require my full eight hours' sleep, and in any case was far too excited getting the place right, inducing electricians and others to do what we wanted, and shopping around for things. I sometimes attempted to catch up on sleep by taking a nap, but was usually too tense and my brain too active, so I soon abandoned that. There was too much to live for, now that I could realise my dream of being an ordinary housewife like anyone else.

Moreover, I had to be available at all times to *mon cher mari* who had irregular hours and was liable to call in at any moment for a quickie. I thought this awfully romantic, and was proud that he needed me physically so much. Not

13

infrequently we had it off three times a day; he was sexually voracious, but then so was I.

Learning to be a housewife was fun. To match his tales from the squadroom, I would recount the major events of my day: how I went on running the vacuum cleaner hose over the carpet without noticing that it had detached itself from the machine, how I left the coffee grinder lid off and spent 20 minutes picking up the beans, how I broke some eggs into the rubbish bin and tried to fry the shells. He would chuckle and toss his head, obviously delighted at having a scatterbrained little wife – his baby doll. As for this soubriquet, I still wished he would find something else as I hated it, but decided after all that it was too small an irritant to tarnish our wonderful life together.

A good deal of my time was spent making sure I looked attractive just in case he called in unexpectedly, which he often did only an hour or so after leaving. My wardrobe was crammed with new clothes.

'You're not bored?' Serge asked once or twice. 'Don't you want to go out a bit – concerts, parties, discos?'

'I'm wonderfully happy as things are,' I replied. At this stage it was only too apparent that all he wanted was his very own bit of skirt to come home to, and I had no objection to that at all. We couldn't get enough sex, and the more we had the more we wanted. He told me he would become roused while working simply thinking of me, and I returned the compliment saying that was why so many eggs found their way into the bin while I daydreamed.

About two months after we got married, Serge went away for a week's special training north of Paris.

I had always been vastly over-sexed just as some people are big eaters or incontinent gamblers. Now I had to exist a whole week without sex! I gritted my teeth but have to confess that I endured the frustration only three days. With my next fuck impossibly far away in time, I had no appetite even for a parsley omelette. Being a loyal soul I went for a long walk in the country on the third day to use up my energy, and returned home limping. I had a cold shower and it only made my withdrawal symptoms worse. I was dying to have it off, and in desperation phoned Serge's barracks outside Paris, but he was busy. So I waited for his regular call at 10 p.m., when I told him it was hell without him, and he chortled that he sincerely hoped so. I said my head was in a whirl and I couldn't concentrate on anything and I was sure I was a nymphomaniac and it was all his fault. He said I shouldn't say such things over the phone even if they were true.

'I'll be back on Monday, it's only four days.'

'But you'll be at work all day I suppose, so that makes five.'

'I'll pop in early in the morning.'

'Oh Serge *chéri*, please do, I'll count the hours. What time in the morning?'

'Whatever you do, don't start drinking. Stick to Coca Cola.'

'All right, Coca Cola it is, but if you don't come back soon I might have to make use of the bottle too!'

We ended the call making lovey-dovey noises at each other and I went into the bathroom and turned the radio on, meaning to wash my hair. Now I couldn't stop thinking of the Coke bottle! I managed to finish my hair without incident and then decided to have a bubble bath, ostensibly in order to achieve relaxation, but in fact with malice aforethought. Ah, how we deceive ourselves when we fall into temptation!

A man with neat, quiet diction on 'France Culture' was talking about films, caressing the listeners in a seductive whisper, which of course was why he had the job – because of his posh drawing-room voice. The instant I turned the taps on and squirted the foam liquid into the bath I knew I was going to give in. The hot viscous water slithered over my skin as I rolled this way and that palming my breasts and abdomen. I should never have taken that country walk, it had simply stirred my senses.

Suddenly my hand movements became more precise and I found myself tweaking my nipples, which sent signals flying to my aching quim. Soon I was massaging myself languidly between my legs, telling myself this was part of my normal ablutions, and that I was only soothing the ache down there. The film chap's sibilant voice articulated every word, now he was swapping little jokes with a woman presenter. I imagined his snow-white teeth and could almost feel his clean breath. My legs parted of their own volition and my insides churned while I watched my thatch floating rhythmically like a tiny sea beast as the bathwater rose and fell.

There was no ambiguity now, I was positively gasping with desire for the man on the radio, doubtless tall and impeccable in an Armani suit and with a flat tummy and a prick as smooth and straight as his 500-franc tie. I pictured him vividly as my fingers slipped between the splayed lips of my cunt, circled the rim and then pushed deeper into the warm haven within. I luxuriated in the friction on the rigid pad of flesh within my tunnel of love.

There was no holding back at this point, and I shamelessly betrayed Serge for Monsieur France Culture, emptying some of the bathwater so that I could make love to myself properly. With my hot zone now fully exposed above the water, I looked about for a lubricant and found a jar of body cream, which I mingled with my natural juices. I lay back waiting for the tang of desire, catching my breath when it began somewhere in my midriff and then spread lower.

I got up and sat on the edge of the bath and had the idea of splaying my bottom, so that slight pain joined the pleasure as my two hands vibrated in my hungry crack. If only the radio man could have been sucking at my breasts, it would have doubled my pleasure. The soles of my feet prickled and I remember screwing up my toes as a surge of delight shot up the back of my knees.

I needed a cock badly, and there it was, the orange shampoo bottle with the round knob. No, it was too hard and unyielding! Running into the kitchen, dripping water all the way, I found a thin aubergine, all satin and shiny and purple. Resuming my position I eased this inside my front passage, then repeatedly withdrew it and pushed it in again. With my free hand I fingered my nipples while the rubbery phallus fucked and fucked me.

Alas, I could not reach my climax this way and, almost in despair, lunged for a towel which I folded and laid on the bath edge. I stood the aubergine upon this and went down on it, rocking back and forth and pummelling my swinging tits. Oh bliss, it was working! Again and again I thrust down on my purple comforter, shuddering in orgasm, ramming the thing in as far as I could, and extracting the last ounce of pleasure from my abused body as the smooth voice of 'France Culture' filled the void between my cries. Afterwards I rinsed myself slowly and shivered.

Guilty but assuaged, I awaited my husband's return. He called from a filling station on the *autoroute* around 7 a.m. on the Monday saying: 'Be with you in 20 minutes.' I brushed my teeth, splashed my face in cold water and made for the kitchen stool.

The kitchen stool? It was often used when Serge called to announce his arrival, which was the signal that he wanted an immediate session with me. Naturally I was not always ready or in the mood, so I would sit bare-bottomed on the stool diddling with myself next to the radiator. By the time I greeted him I was well turned on, and we would plunge into the bedroom, usually after a hasty drink, and he would say *'nom d'un chien*, you come on fast', and I would smile sweetly and say: 'I go weak when I hear the lift on its way.'

One midday before the summer had really begun, he turned up to find me in bed. He had given no warning, and intuitively I suspected trouble.

'What's going on?' he demanded. 'The place is filthy. Are you ill?'

My face and two sets of fingers peeped out at him over the bedclothes: 'They've turned the heating off. Come and join me.'

He put me in my place at once: 'It's not that cold. Hurry up and get busy, I'm starving and I've only got half an hour.' I leapt out obediently and rushed to the refrigerator for eggs. 'And I don't want another flaming omelette!'

Annoyed, I found some left-overs and shoved them in the microwave. Five minutes later I bore the result to him on a tray together with a length of bread, a glass of wine and a napkin. I was still in my nightdress, a shortie with lacy cutaway briefs, and hoped the spectacle would wipe the scowl off his face.

'What is this supposed to be.'

'A sort of goulash.'

'Looks awful. What's the white stuff?'

'Potatoes, they broke up,' I sniffed. I dislike men when they converse like army sergeants. In addition I was barefoot and freezing.

'Hm,' he said, fishing a piece of cork out of his glass. 'About time you learnt to open a bottle. Get me a bowl.'

'You were in a hurry, and I . . .' I went for the bowl, and he solemnly tipped the surplus gravy into it, along with some of the meat.

'That's better,' he barked. I ceased all movement and watched him shovel the food into his mouth. After a bit he looked up, I began an anxious smile, and he added with his mouth full: 'Well, don't stand there catching pneumonia. Put something on.'

Sudden anger shot to the top of my head from somewhere round the small of my back. 'Yes Serge,' I squeaked, hurrying into the bedroom. I realised that I was no longer trembling with fury or the cold, but with a glow of desire, my thoughts strangely excited. His reprimands had actually roused me sexually! To myself, I whispered again: 'Yes Serge, yes my hero.'

To be perfectly honest, the feeling was not new, it had come over me once before at the Top Club when a couple of the members had chastised me. I had remained semiroused for days, and at the time I had seen this turn of events as a glimpse into heaven – the heaven of the masochist!

Brossard relented, bringing his tray back into the kitchen: 'Sorry, *ma biche*, forget what I said. I've had some upsetting news at the office, but I won't bother you with it. The government's sabotaging one of my cases. I'll just

18

have this apple and go. Keep warm, maybe we should have an electric fire for emergencies like this.'

He chomped at the apple and kneaded my neck. I turned to him: 'Can't you stay another ten minutes?'

'Boss wants me, she's in a nasty mood too.'

I blinked: 'Oh I never knew your boss was a woman.'

He did not answer but pecked at my mouth, and I stood at the door with parted lips. My fingers strayed to them, feeling their puckered flesh. For pity's sake, Serge worked for a woman!

He was niggly again a week later, moaning one evening about too much curry in the chicken fricassee: 'Tastes like some Indian cowpat. And this rice is overcooked, you should run it under the cold tap after it's done.'

'I forgot,' I said miserably.

'While we're at it, I wish you'd be careful about brushing your teeth, there's toothpaste everywhere.'

'Oh be reasonable, toothpaste wipes off.'

'Off the ceiling?'

'Anything else while we're at it?'

'Yes. If you insist on putting creases in my pyjamas, put them at the front and not at the sides.'

'How should I know? Anyhow, no self-respecting man wears pyjamas in the 1980's. You should get some night-shirts, *mon vieux*, and stop fussing about nothing.' I took a deep breath and waded into him, my voice rising several semitones: 'You're constantly complaining these days: the washing, the omelettes and the goulash and the chicken and the rice, there's toothpaste on the ceiling and your pyjamas are the wrong way round. Anyone'd think this was a girl guide camp.'

Serge's eyes took on a murderous look: 'Stop that. I get enough petticoat government at work without . . .'

'There's no need to take it out on me, it's not me who's doing the complaining. If you think running a home is easy you should try it for a week or two, and perhaps you wouldn't reduce me to a down-trodden wife. You know what happens to wives like that? They rebel. They rebel

19

and poison, yes poison, their husbands, and . . .' I had flung off my apron and was waving my arms about.

'Oh yes, and how do you propose to deal with the corpse?'

'I'd cut the head off. That's right, I'd cut it off and throw it down the rubbish chute. And if you're worried about the rest, I-I'd take it down the stairs, the back stairs, on a Sunday at half past one when everyone's having lunch. Bump it down step by step and nobody would know. And then I'd leave it in the front hall and at two thirty the children would finish their icecream and find it and tell their parents and everyone would come streaming out into the hall and nobody would know how the headless body got there. Hah! Nobody would even know who the headless body was. So there!' I ended the tirade by putting my tongue out at him.

My prospective victim stormed round the table and dealt me a whopping slap on one cheek. I shrieked with hysterical fright but he followed me with a mighty back-hander on the other cheek and for several seconds I was totally mute. Then I fled into the bathroom, struggling to lock the door. He forced his way in, then somehow got a foot on the edge of the bath and I was across his thigh. He delivered four thwacks to my behind and stormed out, leaving me bawling like a seven-year-old and fighting for air.

Then I stopped suddenly. There it was again, that same exquisite glow and the shaking that went with it. A kind of sour taste was rushing all over me. Wiping off the tear-stains I went into the lounge where Serge had abandoned the meal and was sitting on an upright chair in front of the TV jabbing at the buttons. One look at his stiff neck and flushed ears told me he would never apologise – ever. I went round and faced him.

'I'm sorry, Serge,' I declared meekly. 'I don't know what came over me, I should never have gone on like that. I went mad.' Repentance, fear and desire eddied between my legs. 'I'm sorry,' I repeated.

He did not move but started flicking over the pages of the TV magazine.

'Nothing on the telly,' he muttered. Then he threw the magazine into the grate.

After which he gave me a smile: 'Forget it.' Then he was slamming his mouth against mine, and I was on his lap burying my face in his shoulder and telling him: 'I do love you so, I'd die for you.'

'And I love you, Laure-Anne *mon bijou*, but you need a firm hand.' His fingers were running along my thigh under my skirt, then more purposefully. I held on tightly and gave him bites on his ear.

'I deserved to be smacked,' I ventured. 'If I do wrong again you must punish me.'

He fondled me some more and I purred. He said: 'You wouldn't be a little maso-inclined, by chance?' It had taken him a while to think this up.

'I don't think so. Perhaps.'

Within seconds his trousers were off and my panties were flung aside.

Afterwards he said: 'It's those Christian Dior stockings that do it.'

There was more to it than that, I was beginning to suspect. Possibly a great deal more.

Chapter Three

There could not have been a more compatible couple, I firmly believed. We enjoyed a deep understanding, with Serge quickly growing accustomed to my predilictions in love-making, and I to his.

It was reassuring and flattering to have an every-ready husband, his cock perky at all times, though he was less inventive than I was. On trips into the country, I was the one who selected the hay to romp in, who urged him to make love to me in some village phonebox late at night, who elbowed him into asking for a room for an hour or two while we were lunching at an *auberge*. My physical hunger showed now sign of abating, and even during the long hours on my own I was permanently conscious of my body and the pains and pleasures it underwent.

In leisure and culture we might well have clashed, had I not sensed the danger. To simplify the matter, TV was about all Serge could cope with day by day, because of the stress involved in his job, whereas I had always sought to keep my brain active through broader interests. Actually it worked out well, as I kept my love of painting, Schönberg's music, and my heavy reading to myself. It wasn't that I was a snob, simply that I had always been more disposed to intellectual delights.

However that may be, I readily fell in with his wishes in

the realm of entertainment. We were keen film-goers, which gave us long hours of happiness together. I glowed with pride and smugness on the arm of my handsome husband in the cinema queue, on equal terms with the other wives and sweethearts chattering away with their lovers. This is a humble glory nobody should despise, for the number of suicides attempted by people without a friend in the cinema queue must run into millions. Once inside, Serge and I would sit transfixed holding hands, and it was fun discussing the film afterwards.

But a couple cannot live wrapped up in themselves for any length of time, and the outlines of a social round appeared in June. Neither of us had close bonds with our families and, while my closest friends were the ones I had left behind at Les Chabannes, I knew none of his circle. Rather at my insistence we began exchanging dinners with his coterie. He enjoyed showing me off, people were very nice to me and I think they liked me. On the other hand I was reluctant to invite my girl friends, partly because they did not blend in with the kind of normal world I was hoping we could create, and partly from a natural fear of introducing my man to attractive women.

In this connection I must mention my first encounter with The Widow, a copper-haired woman of about 35 who had lost her policeman husband in a gunfight early that year. She twitched her head and mouth when she spoke and proved both touchy and snooty.

'Financially,' she told me at our flat-warming party, which had got off to an auspicious start when a joker stuck price tags on the buffet dishes, 'I have nothing to complain of, as the insurance took care of the house. It's a huge place on the edge of Pontambert. I play records to drown the creaking of furniture at night. People stop by, though, mostly Marcel's old colleagues. Serge pops in occasionally.'

This was news to me, and she said it so deliberately. 'Yes, of course,' I mumbled.

'I suppose you're gloriously happy with him. He's so handsome.'

'So far so good.' I tried not to look too elated.

'And he's lucky to find an ex-hostess,' she said cattily.

'I wasn't exactly . . .'

'He's one of my old flames.'

'Was, not is, I hope. I'm sure you had plenty of choice.'

'Do I look that broken down?'

I laughed: 'Oh no, I only meant you're very attractive, you have a good figure.'

'I trained for ballet, you know. But don't worry about Serge, he's yours now, and it's early days. I *still* have plenty of choice.'

'I'd like to come and see you, perhaps some afternoon. I've always hoped I'd have a lovely house in the country some day.'

'We must arrange it. Bring Serge, he can mow the lawn.'

But she made no attempt to set a date, and I fled to the other guests.

Not long afterwards I had my first real punishment from Serge. It was on a Saturday, I remember, and for reasons known only to himself my dearly-beloved woke in a perfectly foul mood, clumping about at the crack of dawn making breakfast, which was normally my exclusive preserve. I left him to it and we had our coffee and toast in bed. I thanked him sweetly, but he was still jumpy and soon vacated our snug sheets and began to inspect the flat in the manner of an insurance assessor.

'You could have changed the water in the flowers, they stink,' he yelled from the living room. I made no reply. 'There's dust all over the hi-fi.' What could I say? 'This broken plate in the dustbin, good thing it's not one of the dinner service.' Later: 'The clasp has snapped on your pearl bracelet.' I said: 'The cat made off with it and we had a tug of war. Will it cost much to get it fixed?'

His voice had been rising and now he was shouting: 'I'll see if I can do it. But all this is very annoying, you're letting yourself go, the place looks like a flea market. Get out of bed! Come here!' Clad in white tennis shorts and wine-red polo neck shirt he lectured me: 'You have nothing to do all day, and you still manage to make a mess of it. I've been watching you lately, Laure-Anne, and your behaviour is getting worse: slipshod cleaning, sloppy meals, dust and dirt everywhere. Come here.' I took a step closer. 'I'm afraid you need a sharp lesson, you must be punished for slackness and your whole attitude to your duties. You asked me to, didn't you? Didn't you?'

'Yes, Serge.'

'Stand over there by the bookshelf with your hands on your head. *Facing* the wall, you ninny! Keep your hands there.' Then came a longish pause while he clicked a cassette into place, some punk thing with a bullwhip beat. 'Fetch a coat hanger, a wooden one.' This I did. 'Now close the curtain.' I obeyed and stood before him waiting, my hands once more on my head and facing the wall.

We were crossing the Rubicon. Reading and reflection since those days have led me to the essential conclusion that there are two kinds of sado-masochism: the sort indulged in for fun and kicks, usually by the superior classes in clubs or private gatherings, and the genuine kind – ours. For this intercourse to make any sense there must be no choice for the victim, and the practices must satisfy both parties, otherwise the relationship is merely a straightforward absence of compatibility, leading to divorce or some other litigation; alternatively the slave just walks out. I am being rather scientific about this, but it does explain subsequent events.

In our case, once the power struggle had begun, I could either stand up to him and argue every point, from how to open a pack of butter to the right way to place the hall rug, or else I could accept the humiliations Serge so clearly had a taste for administering. Furthermore, I was sincerely head over heels in love with my husband and on no account could I bear the prospect of losing him. I truly acknowledged him as the most wonderful guy in the world, the one and only person I would follow to the ends of the earth. From that point onwards, whatever Serge said or did was fine by me.

'I am going to beat you, Laure-Anne,' he was saying. 'But it is for your own good, it is because I love you, you understand. You realise that?'

'Yes, Serge. You know I love you, I deserve to be beaten, but I would never allow anyone else to do it.'

He cleared his throat: 'How many strokes do you think you should have?'

'I don't know.'

'Don't be childish, how many?'

'I haven't done anything very bad. Four?'

'Six, I think, in view of your general indolence.'

He told me to turn round and face him, and my eyes shot to the bulge in his tennis shorts. In the half-light he pulled out one of the straight-backed chairs from the dining table. 'Kneel on that. You can have this cushion under your middle. Now bend over the back of the chair and hold on to the uprights. That's it, right over.'

He moved next to me to 'help' me bend over, and the bump in his shorts pressed into my bottom. There was a delay while he tucked a second chair the other way under the cushion to prevent me toppling forward, and this gave him another excuse for nudging his cock into my arse. He then hitched up my shortie nightdress and tugged my cutaway panties tighter, the material pulling up between the spheres of my buttocks. I dared not look round.

'Now keep still and don't make a noise. You don't want the neighbours to know you are being smacked in this degrading manner. And take your hands away or they'll get hurt. I was taking in short breaths and expelling the air slowly each time. 'Now, my girl, this will soon be over.' I winced when the coathanger touched me as he took aim, and then the first stroke fell with a sharp crack, hitting me with immense force and making me grip the chair legs with all my might. It stung more fiercely than I had imagined it would, and I said hoarsely, 'On no, Serge I . . .' But as the second smack came I sucked in my lips.

'Keep quiet,' he said, 'it's no use thinking you'll be let off.'

I knew he was leering at me, maybe wishing he could give me lots of strokes, perhaps wondering whether he could go the whole way and thrash me dozens of times until he came. I could picture his penis stretching his shorts, and the frustration he was suffering and could not act upon. The third stroke cut viciously into my bottom and I knew I was right. Instinctively I forced my rear up and worked my back up and down, trying fruitlessly to tense my muscles and lessen the pain.

Three more to come, and these would sting wickedly as he got into his stride. Again I thought of his mounting excitement and this gave me the will to continue offering myself as his helpless victim. It was the fifth stroke that hurt most, because the coathanger struck my thighs, and I released a sharp cry. The bastard! But there was only one more and it would be over.

I waited but nothing happened, except for a rustle that told me he was dropping his shorts, and then his underpants. He approached and grasped my waist, fiddling with the elastic round my middle and feeling for my gusset, his penis lying hot and stiff in my rear crack. He was snorting like a bull but eventually he moved away and the sixth stroke lashed into me, causing me to yell through my puckered lips.

'One extra for crying out,' he ruled. It was worse than anything so far, and I squealed in pain.

My head hung loose and I was shaking so much that the chairs rattled. I heard him put his shorts on again.

'Now you may get up,' he said in a curiously weak voice. I unbent and stood swaying, staring at the chairs. The cushion dropped to the floor. 'Come here.' He spun me round and ordered me to lower my panties 'slowly'. He inspected my stripes for a long time and concluded: 'That will be all. What do you say?'

'Thank you Serge,' I whispered thickly, and he threw the coathanger onto the settee. A pyramid was sticking out in front of his shorts, and I looked at it in silence. His face was scarlet and, grimly he pulled me to him, to kiss me fervently with his hardness digging into my belly, the sweat patches on his shirt warm and damp against me.

'Love me, *mon prince*,' I groaned, my mouth following his.

'Laure-Anne, my own Laure-Anne,' he said, his fingers craftily feeling for the weals he had produced.

He took my hand, inviting me to grope him, then I tugged his arm and guided him to the bedroom where we tumbled onto the rumpled sheets and he ploughed into me.

Chapter Four

My vacuum-cleaner hated me, and the feeling was mutual.

Serge phoned to say he'd be leaving the office in one minute. I took the call dripping with bathwater, and had to rush about tidying up. Part of this involved running the Electrolux over the rug in the hall, and at one point I opened the door and ran the machine over the mat on the landing. The cat decided to make a bid for freedom, I hurled the cleaner back into the flat and chased after Cucu. Whereupon the door closed behind me blown by the through draught from the open kitchen window. The lift came up.

'What are you doing naked on the landing holding the cat?'

'Well nothing really. It can happen to anyone.'

Another time he came storming home, having learned through the office that the fire brigade had come to the flat when the washing machine overflowed and I didn't know where the stopcocks were.

We also had the brilliant idea of putting a blind up at the kitchen window, but neither of us could understand the instructions.

'You hold it and I'll mark up the holes,' the man of the house suggested. 'Where's the pencil got to?'

'Over here,' I enthused, letting the blind drop.

'Hold the blind, I'll get the pencil.'

'Are you sure this is the proper way round? Shouldn't the blind roll next to the window?'

'Where else would it roll?'

'On the floor like it just did. Ha-ha-ha.'

'Hold this flange.'

'I've only got two hands. What's the flange for?'

'Holding up the blind.'

'But I'm already holding it up.'

'When it's in place, nuthead!'

'When what's in place?'

'*Mon dieu*, the blind! Now, is this flange at a right angle?'

'Looks all right to me, it's parallel anyway.'

'It can't be parallel and at a right angle at the same time.'

'It can if it's parallel with the other wall.'

'What wall?'

'That one over there,' I wailed, shaking with helpless laughter.

'But we're putting it on this wall here. God give me patience.'

'You're telling me. I'm the one holding up the goddam blind, and I'm being very patient. My arms are aching. You should try to be more patient, too, or we'll never get it done. If you don't know how to do it, we should call someone in.'

Not all our quarrels were so light-hearted. I asked him, for example, if I could go out and look for a part-time job.

'Certainly not,' was his retort. 'I can earn for both of us.'

'I know you can, *chéri*,' I replied. 'What I mean is I don't have enough to occupy my mind. A job would give me an interest. Couldn't you wangle me a nice receptionist job? You're away a lot, evenings quite often, and I need an outlet. My brain might go soft.'

He would have none of it: 'An outlet in the evening? I don't want you running the streets, I need you here. I could come staggering in at any time with a bullet in my shoulder!'

'Huh?'

'You know perfectly well what I mean. Your job is here.

30

I can't have you, smothered in perfume, dolled up in some dentist's office. A girl like you is a magnet, and I'm making sure you don't start attracting men, especially if they've got bad teeth.'

The discussion was becoming involved, but I persisted: 'I go out already, shopping and chatting with neighbours and such. I could pick up a man any day I like. What's the difference?'

'What's the difference!'

'I didn't mean it like that, *mon amour*. I'll never look at another man and you know that. You just don't trust me, and that's unfair. I trust *you*.' I put on my steamiest pout.

He growled back: 'You're staying right here. It's the men I don't trust. There's too much talk in this town already.'

'Well,' I said, 'if anyone knows how to handle men, it's me.'

'That's what I'm afraid of.'

'Lots of women go out to work to have a purpose. I know there are two sides to an argument but they can't both be yours. You're always complaining I'm an idiot, but you're turning me into one. Be fair.'

Subsequently I announced that I was going to join a body-building club that had just started up. He said I was nicely put together already and I finished up with an exercise bike in the cellar.

A few more scuffles along these lines, and then Serge began to mope. The last thing I intended was to wreck our marriage with a major row over secondary issues, so I capitulated. From now on I would agree with everything he said, would simply be Brossard's fluffy little wife, always smiling at everyone, laughing at the men's jokes, listening wide-eyed as they put the country and the planet to rights, soaking up the women's gossip. Didn't I want Serge to be the strong man? Didn't I get a little thrill every time I was obliged to give in?

The punishment sessions continued from time to time, and for the flimsiest of reasons: further breakages, the wheel of the keep-fit bike rubbing against a wine rack and smashing a bottle (which I threw away, but the wine patch remained in evidence), failing to defrost the fridge (how was I to know?). Serge instituted a system of black marks, an outrageously one-sided procedure that had me standing with my hands on my head for 30 minutes at a time, crawling around the lounge wearing only stockings and a waspie, being thrown across the settee arm and whacked with a belt or a ruler.

Once he overdid this and drew blood. I had gone out leaving some things in the bathroom sink with the tap on, and the boss arrived for lunch to find me once again struggling with dishcloths, towels and bowls. There was water everywhere, it ran a yard into the living room, and Serge went raving mad, grabbing his belt and thrashing me unmercifully so that I flew into a genuine panic and shrieked with pain and terror. Later I was horrified at the thick pink weals on my bottom, one of which had a red streak at one end.

There was an awkward sequel to this.

Two days later I had a phone call from the woman across the landing, inviting me in for coffee. Still sore, and on the whole pretty fed up, I accepted.

Diane Bazillac and I had walked to the shops together several times and had the odd drink. She had always seemed rather forbidding, not least because her husband was a local councillor and owned half a street in the town. About 40, Diane was tall with a tendency to droop at the shoulders like some of the more absurd fashion models, and she wore mostly trouser suits or jeans. She had a longish face, sharp features and a straight mouth. Her golden hair was swept back and tied with a black ribbon. From her la-di-da accent and haughty manner one was presumably expected to deduce that she had married beneath her. I doubted whether I would ever warm to her.

'I hate afternoons,' she said, leading me into a lounge done out in furniture from the Gironde region where papa had a 30-room chateau. 'They are neither one thing or the other and they drag so.'

'Most people are at a low ebb in the afternoon.'

'I like having someone in. Hubert says I should do aerobics or something, but I'm not the sort. It's such a business keeping to a time-table.' She poured out coffee and cut a fruit cake. 'I usually buy cakes, but I did this one specially for us.'

I enthused over it, and she went on: 'How do you fill in the afternoons? You told me you do your chores in the morning.'

'Oh, I stay in reading or catching up on sleep mostly.'

Diane gave the suspicion of a leer: 'Ah of course, you being newly-weds.'

'Four months.'

'No babies on the way?'

'Give us a chance. I'd like to start a family but . . .'

'He's against it, most men are, they're too calculating. Hubert and I never had any children, he sort of went off sex. Are your people in this area?'

'No. Neither of us has much contact with our families.'

'Sad.'

There was a pause and I volunteered: 'Serge doesn't hit it off with his mother – she's widowed and living in Paris – because she nagged his dad to an early death. But I'd better not go into that.'

'And you?'

'My people are mostly in the Paris suburbs. They more or less disowned me when I became a club hostess and then launched my own place.' I found a spot for my plate on the coffee table.

'Ooh I say, I never knew,' Diane cooed, slinking over to squat next to me on the sofa and easing the table away. 'How intriguing, you must go on!' I dealt with this as succinctly as I could, but her tongue was hanging out for details.

'Do tell me, you must have seen everything in those clubs. And done everything too, I mean I don't want to jump to conclusions, but after all that's what clubs are for.'

Her conclusions were exactly right, and I evaded the question: 'I was only *la patronne* at Les Chabannes.'

'You must know lots of scandal, everything that was going on.'

'I did the accounts and supervised the place. What people got up to was their affair.' I was becoming angry, and was within a hair's breadth of telling her off. She felt this and switched the conversation.

'And now you are married. Do have another slice, another cup perhaps?' I accepted. 'That's a sweet dress, Laure-Anne, a lovely shade of green, pleats too, they're nice. I adore pleats, but on others, I'm too gaunt and they always look so dreary on me.' Handing me the cup and saucer, which occupied both my hands, she ran a hand over the pleats, then an arm along my shoulder. 'What an extraordinary figure you have, your husband must be proud of you.'

I smiled: 'Oh yes he is. We're deeply in love.'

'I'm sure you are. Can't keep his hands off you. No wonder you need a nap in the afternoons. We could have one together.' She waved her hand nonchalantly and giggled.

I wished we could talk about astrology or *nouvelle cuisine*. She kept fingering my neckline, and my suspicions were roused.

'Quite a party you had the other evening.'

'Party?' I gaped.

'People screaming and shouting.' I went crimson. She said: 'Oh dear, I think I've gaffed. I didn't mean to be nosy, I just thought I heard fireworks or something. A kind of popping noise.'

I laughed: 'That was Serge repairing a – er, I mean doing some upholstery.'

We both knew I was lying, and she charged on: 'He beats you, I can tell.' I had no chance to deny it. 'Hubert used to do that, and if the truth be known I learnt to like it. I expect you do, too. Hubert tired of it, gave it up. He's given up practically everything. I sometimes wonder whether he hasn't turned homo.'

Her forceful probing did not entirely surprise me, for during our trips she had already emerged as one of those expansively talkative women for whom no subject is taboo. In conversation, she had successively cut down to size President Mitterrand, the local mayor, the pope and the Supreme Soviet of the USSR among others. It was her style, and I now sought to counter-attack by showing up her disgraceful prattling.

'I'm so sorry, Diane, I had no idea of course, but you can rest assured that your private affairs are safe with me.'

She gave a shrug: 'Even if he does have his young men, I'm not short of girlfriends. You only live once. Win or lose, I'm determined to have a good time before the wrinkles come. How encouraging to meet someone with similar ideas.'

I could only stare at her impeccably cut, black summer trousers with their knife-edge creases, topped by an off-white speckled blouse with puffy sleeves. She was appallingly overbearing, but I had to admit she carried it off with the utmost poise.

'Do tell me,' she gushed, squeezing my hand, 'have you ever done it with another woman?'

'Really Diane, don't you think we're letting our hair down rather too much?'

'Ah, so you have. How wonderful.'

'You're completely off-track,' I squeaked. 'I prefer men, as it happens. Now I'm afraid I must go. My husband is due in at six and he'll be starving.'

We both got up and she blurted out: 'I don't care, I'm going to say it, Laure-Anne. I want you, I've been trying to make you for weeks, ever since I met you, I . . .'

A moment's hesitation, and she seized my arms, held them to my sides and pulled me to her, her mouth closing on mine taking me completely off guard. She kissed me hard, hugging me with the strength of a man, her thrusting chin digging into one side of my mouth. I jerked a leg up but she imprisoned that, too, between her thighs. I was suffocating and my lips parted, she held them like that with her mouth and insinuated the warm flesh of her tongue. I struggled to escape, but it only excited her more and she rubbed her breasts against mine.

35

I tried and failed to get a hand-hold on her mass of hair. Finally my mouth came free: 'No please! I'm not that sort, I don't want it, you're hurting me, let me go, let me go!' Our pubic bones were still clamped tight together, and her hands clutched my buttocks.

'I won't hurt you, anything but that,' she panted. 'Oh God, you're so nice and cuddly! Don't be angry.' Suddenly she released me. 'I had to try, I simply had to, somehow I hoped you might, I had to try, please understand. Don't go, don't go, let me explain. Please Laure-Anne!'

'I think you've explained enough for one afternoon,' I replied hotly.

She collapsed on the settee. 'One minute, that's all I ask, I'll never touch you again, I swear it. If you only knew how agonisingly difficult it is in a town this small. I've had to be so careful. And when you moved in, I thought, I hoped . . . You are so lovely and feminine and for weeks your fragrance has been driving me mad, not your perfume, your natural scent. Oh, *ma chérie*, I'm so impulsive. When we were standing so close a minute ago, I knew it was my only chance, whatever the consequences. And now I've messed it all up. We can stay friends, can't we?'

My anger was fading at the sight of her tears. I said: 'I do understand, Diane, and I appreciate your honesty. In fact I have slept with other women, two to be exact. To be perfectly frank, I enjoyed it with one and not with the other.' I took a step nearer. 'I do sympathise, but I made a choice a long time ago, I'm hetero and will never go back on that. We'll stay friends, I want us to. Thank you for saying such nice things about me, but it's no good. If Serge ever found out you'd so much as kissed me, he'd disfigure me for life.'

She glanced up with a strangely warped smile: 'He'd whip you again, and you'd like it, you're the sort.'

I raised my eyebrows, trying to adopt a kind tone: 'He loves me, you must understand, and I worship him. We can't change that. But I promise you my lips are sealed. This never happened, as far as I'm concerned.'

I made for the door, but she said harshly: 'Not for me,

it isn't over. You're the chance of a lifetime for me, Laure-Anne, I'll woo you and win you. I've nothing to lose – nothing at all!' She made a wild grab at me and I scrabbled for the latch. 'I'll tell Serge!' she snapped.

I froze: 'Tell him what?'

'That we are in love, that we spent the afternoon together. Don't look so naive.'

'Naive! Well of all the cheek! You must be completely out of your mind. Do you realise he'd come in here and blow a hole through your head!'

'He wouldn't,' she smirked, 'not if I told him it was your idea, that you tried to have it off with me. He'd blow a hole in *your* head. He knows your past record!'

I was open-mouthed: 'That's blackmail! He'd never believe you! What record? Have you been discussing me with him?'

'He'd believe me all right. A ripped dress, a broken vase, a phone call to his office, a hysterical call saying I was lodging a complaint for assault. Your word against mine, *ma chérie.*'

Salt tears of fury stabbed at my eyes and my vision grew blurred. The bitch! In my newfound innocence I had so longed for a simple existence, and now this up-market dyke was spoiling it all, and had the effrontery to call it love.

Bazillac's eyes narrowed, and she knew she had won. She stood up and with a smile produced a hankie. I refused it and whirled round.

'I'm going,' I muttered.

'Of course. But you must come back tomorrow. You can have two lovers, Serge and me. Why not? I want you to come back tomorrow.'

I was within an ace of telling Serge everything, for I was frightened enough to need a father confessor. But it so happened that he came in late buckling at the knees with exhaustion from working 14 hours non-stop on a case, wanting only a quick snack and a long sleep.

'Sorry, *ma biche,*' he said with genuine regret. 'We're on a drug watch, stake out at dawn tomorrow, tip-off from

Saint-Raphael. I think I'm heading for a cold.' Geisha-like I waited on my hero, fed him, undressed him and put him to bed like a child.

It was a restless night for me, and when Serge got up to make his own breakfast at 5 a.m. I still did not know what I was going to do about La Bazillac. There was no question just now of raising the problem with Serge, and I sent him off happy before scuttling back between the sheets and catching up on a couple of hours' slumber.

All that morning I was undecided, but at 2 p.m. she phoned and I said I would join her in 15 minutes. She asked me to wear a blue pleated skirt and I said I only had a black one.

She could be a dangerous enemy, and no doubt I was dramatising the whole business. With luck the tryst might turn out to be a one-off affair, in which case I would be laughing at the ridiculous episode three months hence. Arguably, I might as well lie back and enjoy it, and by the time I crossed the landing I had virtually convinced myself that I was doing this for Serge, even saving him from the wrath of Councillor H. Bazillac.

From my limited experience with other women, I knew that the best fantasy was simply to imagine that the other woman was a man. With Butch Bazillac that should be easy as she was half a head taller than I was, and obviously heedless of my feelings and the harm she might do me. I meant to be sure she did none.

She greeted me in fawn leather trousers and a man's striped shirt, and wore no accessories of any kind, not even a wedding ring. I myself had selected a simple white blouse to go with my black skirt, and underneath wore entirely white things with lots of lace edging. I could have made up heavily, but avoided this on the hunch that she preferred the fresh innocent look. Even so I had picked out my most alluring honey-coloured stockings, writing them off already as a total loss. My shoes were high-heeled with buckles and were killing me, but I supposed I would not be wearing them for long.

'I've mixed a little cocktail for us,' Diane announced, handing me a well-filled glass. 'It's a Brazilian mixture and I won't tell you the ingredients.' As long as there was no cyanide I was indifferent to the contents; if it made me tipsy so much the better! We swallowed the drink without ceremony, and I remarked that it was jolly powerful.

'Highly aphrodisiac,' she beamed, setting her glass down. 'Kiss me.' We embraced, and I returned her kiss, giving her a big smile. She was clearly more on edge than I was, but this was her idea and it was up to her to do the spadework.

Diane gabbled on a bit about my clothes, my hair, how I held my head and walked and moved, about my musky fragrance. The curtains were drawn and I slyly cast about in search of a camera or tape recorder. Had I found either, I would have walked out instantly.

'Who were the other two?' she enquired casually, kneeling before me. I told her about a room-mate called Annick, the one I had enjoyed, and Blandine at Les Chabannes, who was also a good friend in spite of her forcing me to have sex with her in return for putting money into my club. All the while, Diane was playing with my skirt, fondling the pleats and even my shoes. At length she put the hem of the skirt to her lips in an act of adoration, then uncovered my knees to kiss and lick them. She rubbed her cheeks between them. I put a hand on her brow.

'Move forward,' she whispered. 'Sit on the edge, I want to look up, that's right. I went to La Visitation college, you know. I used to have the smaller girls when I was a monitor, and was almost expelled for it.' As she rattled on, her fingers fluttered at my stocking tops and at the lace of my knickers. Then she had her head under the skirt and her busy lips were sniffing at their target. I could hear her snorting like a steam-engine, and my own breathing quickened as her expert feather-like touches crept along the outside of my thighs. There was no denying my rising excitement, she was doing it so well.

'My word, you're sizzling already, we both are, I'm almost coming, it's unbelievable.' She pulled away and

39

adroitly squirmed out of her trousers, revealing a pair of tiny glossy green briefs. She made me stand up and my skirt was soon a heap on the floor, while, at her request, I undid her bow and her hair fell about her face, now white and tense with desire.

We were both trembling when we reached the bedroom. With infinite care she laid me on my back and bestowed kisses all over my legs. 'Say nothing, let yourself go.' She rolled me over and continued running her mouth over the backs of my legs. I made little noises of delight, she was so skilled at it. Finally she turned me over again onto my back and pushed my knees up, her wide mouth smiled in delight as she eased my sopping panties down my legs. Then she dived for my quim. Her mouth engulfed my whole sex, her agile tongue lapping me urgently in long, slushy licks from the pereneum – the no-man's-land behind the vulva – to the clitoris. I lifted my crotch, willing her to suck my clit but, maddeningly, she declined.

Instead she gave a low laugh, lisping: 'I say Brossard, you're leaking fast. Naughty little girl, do you like this? Does it give you a nice feeling? You mustn't tell the house mistress, not even another girl, or I'll pay you back. There you are, I'm sure you're coming, I can taste your come. Say you want it, say "please give it to me Diane." '

'Please give it to me, Diane, oh please . . .'

'We haven't time, it's your maths lesson in ten minutes. Wipe yourself.'

'Oh no,' I whimpered, responding to her invention. 'There's still time, I can be late.'

'Do you love me, Brossard?'

'Oh yes, Diane, I do love you. Do it for me, please.'

In reward, she lapped at me again, circling my clit then sucking it hard. A spasm came and I relaxed luxuriously. Diane had miraculously curved her long torso around my body and she guided my hand to her own cleft, warm and big and sopping. I found her clitoris which seemed enormous, actually hanging down. Now she was blowing all over the zone between my legs, and suddenly we were both on our knees, working our hands frantically at each

40

other's slits, then scrabbling at our blouses, clawing at our buttocks and then wanking each other again – doing anything that would augment the utter lewdness of it all. Diane found my mouth and her jutting jaw hurt me as it dug in greedy and insistent.

Alas, at the crucial moment she pulled away, stealing my climax.

'Don't stop!' I cried.

'Get dressed, Brossard, you'll be late for maths and I'll have to report you.'

'You're beastly to me, just because you're a monitor.'

'All right, just this once I'll let you off. D'you want me to make you come, you wicked child?'

'Oh please!'

'Take your blouse off.' I was fast winding down, but I obeyed with alacrity. Now we were both naked except for the stockings that I was wearing. These were Diane's big fetish apparently, for she sat on one of my stockinged thighs and rubbed herself up and down, her middle heaving without restraint as she pleasured herself. She knelt back to change to my other thigh and for the first time I had a full view of her twat – a splayed and meaty gash. She masturbated some more on my other thigh, then got us sitting knees up and face to face so that our quims were touching; they made tiny squelching noises as Diane somehow managed to get our clits in contact.

Then, with her eyes seemingly twice their normal size and her face wet and trembling, she suddenly cried out: 'I'm coming, oh yes I can feel it, my God I'm going to die!' She spread my legs and squashed her vulva onto mine, bucking madly as I, too, fought for a climax, then she went limp and collapsed on top of me, her mouth slobbering against mine. I quickly faked a climax, gyrating furiously.

A few minutes later, still fascinated by my stockings which she stroked lovingly again and again, she whispered conspiratorially: 'Tell me Laure-Anne, do you masturbate?'

I had really had enough of her for one day, so I replied simply: 'I have been known to.'

She mused: 'I do it all the time, always have done. I

41

simply must have relief quickly and often. I suppose its equivalent to premature ejaculation in boys. In fact it was my elder brother who introduced me to the practice; he eventually became Communications Minister.' Her eyes suddenly glazed over and settled on some point behind me: 'From now on, I shall think of you every time.'

Diane Bazillac was a character and a half. Domineering, loquacious and silly, a victim of her own powerful sexual urges, she was a lonely woman perhaps heading for a very sad future.

It was with special care that I showered on return to the flat, glad after all that I had failed to reach an orgasm with her, vowing that there would be no repeat performance. The wretched business would have to stop there. I had yielded to blackmail almost without thinking, but if she tried anything more I would tell her I had confessed to Serge and that he had forgiven me.

Whether I *would* actually inform him was another matter. It was obvious that Diane would be mad to put pressure on a police officer's wife who had 'sneaked' to him and got away with it.

On the other hand she was such a maniac for sex and had the hots for me so badly that she might be prepared to risk everything to satisfy her gargantuan desires.

Chapter Five

It was unfortunate that my second brush with Liliane, the policeman's widow, should have been on the pavement outside a dress shop when I was loaded with parcels. It gave her the perfect excuse for a few digs, and we sparred fiercely.

Having abandoned any semblance of mourning, she wore a shantung off-white ensemble with a gathered bodice, and a long slit down the front of the skirt that showed most of her legs when she walked a brash style that was all the rage at the time.

'Laure-Anne, *ma chère*!'

'Liliane!'

'Spending all your husband's hard-earned pay, I see.'

'Well no, actually, it's from my secret supply. He spends so much on gambling and smokes three packets of cigarettes a day, he can't spare a thing for me.'

Unsure whether I was being funny, she drawled: 'He never used to smoke, it must be the stress. I notice he's put on weight round the middle.'

'Observant of you.'

'Too much office work, I expect. He should take exercise. How about you, d'you do any?'

'I've never felt the need. If ever I did I would know I was ill, and the best thing then is to lie down, any doctor knows that. How are *your* muscles?' I deliberately glared through the skirt slit at a point five centimetres below her crotch. 'You're looking surprisingly vivacious in that eye-catching outfit.'

'*Une folie*, darling. But I've so many dresses now, I'm giving things away. I'll look out a couple for you if you care to come over.'

'They might just suit me. I'd like to try them if I come.'

'We must arrange it.'

Which went to show that, contrary to male belief, women never talk to no purpose. They are always up to some mischief, and whatever it was in Liliane's case I was not intending to help her by jumping to conclusions. I would keep my suspicions to myself and a keener eye on Serge.

Each of us had a chequebook, but it was Serge who ticked off the stubs of both when the monthly bank statements arrived. In fact, he did all the accounts.

'Can you spare a minute?' he yelled through to the kitchen one Sunday morning.

'Just finishing,' I cried gaily, turning down the *blanquette de veau* and sliding a saucepan to one side of the hob. I found him at the dining table glumly flicking over some stubs, and my pearly-toothed smile changed to an anxious swallow. The fire looked cosy, though, and I squatted down in my wifely apron to shift a log, an unnecessary ploy which I suppose a psychiatrist would classify as an anticipatory defence move.

'Take this chair,' he commanded, ignoring the cheery flicker and my alluring knees. 'We are spending too much and I've been going over these cheques of yours. Do you honestly need 5,000 francs a month for housekeeping? Besides, there are dozens of household items paid for by cheque: 215 francs for dry cleaning, 130 francs for drinking glasses, 182 francs for logs, 235 francs for vacuum cleaner repairs, 248 francs for dry cleaning again.' I looked with interest at the offending stubs. 'Half-year insurance for your car – 660 francs, puncture – 80 francs, new battery – no amount stated. Costly privilege a second car, it seems.'

'Oh, but I do use it.'

'About twice a month, not counting kerb-crawling.'

'What!'

'Window shopping by car.'

'It's cheaper if I don't get out,' I replied, flashing him a cheeky smile that died an instant death.

He questioned me about a jumper, a pair of shoes, a cocktail dress and some undesignated items which I tried to identify. 'What's this 325 francs for a restaurant? Which restaurant?'

'Le Moulin des Templiers, with Diane, we take it in turns to pay.'

'Not any more you don't.'

'I agree to that,' I said curtly.

I withdrew from the contest and saw to the meal, which we ate more or less in silence. After that my resident auditor plopped onto the settee and ordered me to stand in front of him. The verdict fell, comprising three sentences to run concurrently or whatever: 1) My car would be sold, 2) My chequebook was to be withdrawn, 3) My allowance was reduced to 3,500 francs a month in cash for housekeeping and 600 francs for myself.

'You're being very mean,' I spluttered. 'Every woman has a chequebook these days, it's humiliating.'

'It's humiliating for me too when the bank phones to say we're insolvent.'

'They haven't!'

'Not yet. But remember, I'm the one earning those figures in the right hand column.'

'And I'm the one who financed the flat!'

'Past history. Anyhow, half of it is yours automatically.'

'Thanks for nothing. The hall, the kitchen and the bathroom, I suppose.'

'I'm acting in your own interest,' he said. 'No, don't creep away. Do you realize that your cheques for the past nine weeks total the princely sum of 20,563 francs and 17 centimes?'

I stood shifting from one leg to the other, my neck prickling with guilt: 'Don't scold me, Serge, I really am surprised. But let me keep my little car. Why can't you just spank me instead? I'd prefer that.'

'Nothing would give you greater pleasure, I'm sure, but the car must go.' He put his arms out for me. 'Now be a good girl and close the curtain, you're giving me a hard-on just wriggling about.' The interview terminated with a post-prandial blow-job.

It's true that finances are indeed never simple and straightforward, unless you are fortunate enough to be lining up in rags at the soup kitchen. For most people there's only the grim compromise and fuss. There was no point in little me worrying as well as Serge and the bank but, as I leaned back against his knees there was no denying that I was showing a big loss. Not only was I now to be dependent on Serge for money, I had lost my mobility and was also being refused permission to have an outside activity. I was resentful that, in return for my loyalty, Serge was denying me that basic human right to earn money and spend it. He was turning into a stuffy old miser, and obviously had a genuinely cruel streak in his make-up. One day he might tire of me and dump me at the bus stop with a 100 franc note! My anguish eventually wore off. After all, I told myself not having any responsibility was a kind of freedom. Moreover, there couldn't be anything seriously wrong with Serge because he knew an awful lot of people and seemed popular, which always reassures a wife.

One chilly October evening I found myself entertaining at dinner two couples of certain note – Georges Bussy, a high-ranking official in the Banque de France, accompanied by his wife Marguerite; and Sylvain Hersin-Coupigny (SHC to close aides and friends), a leading light in the Front National far right party, and his wife Marie-Claire who claimed to be a Royalist and liked to be known as Claire because it went better with her husband's hyphenated sur-name. The dinner party remains firmly in my mind as the first occasion on which our rather mild sado-masochism was laid bare to others. Hitherto I had naturally assumed that what went on within our walls was our own little secret, and it didn't amount to much anyway by some standards.

I had admitted nothing even to Diane Bazillac when she tried to trick me into it, and I would never have dreamed of disclosing our sexual habits to the outside world. Every woman likes secrets, but prefers to discuss those of others.

'I want you to be specially nice to Sylvain,' Serge briefed me. 'I'll fill you in on him and for God sake keep quiet if we talk politics, which we surely will. He's pretty much the frivolous aristocrat, but he's a new power in the land, whatever one's own views. He is also rather special in his tastes and about a year ago interfered with a secretary in a corridor at Avallon town hall. The girl came into the Commissariat next day and I took her statement. I talked her round and she agreed to drop the complaint provided SHC formally apologised to her right there in the squad room. He thanked me warmly and has been chummy with me ever since. I have to play him along in view of his influence – he owns the CFY pulp and paper empire, and is the main shareholder in the Caquelin press group among other things. The Bussys . . .'

'I know him. He was a member of Les Chabannes for two weeks, until his wife found out.'

That evening Serge managed to get home early, and was even kind enough to run to the shops for some things I needed. By 7 p.m. I had the meal about ready and took myself off, later emerging neatly made up and wearing a smart dress that I calculated would surely do him a credit. I was taken aback when Serge announced he had a special dress for me and ordered me to change into it.

'You could have told me,' I whined. 'I'll be late now.'

'I didn't realise you were changing. I got it specially.'

Amazed, I said: 'Let me see it then.'

In the bedroom he gave me a white gold-trimmed tunic with an antique kind of belt made of cord and bronze metal bits.

'Oh, I had no idea it was fancy dress tonight,' I squeaked.

'It isn't,' he said oddly, himself looking like a millionaire in his dark blue suit, white shirt and red and grey striped tie. 'But I want you to wear it.'

'Well all right, but look, it comes halfway up my thighs. When I sit down . . .'

'And white underclothes please, those tailored shorts with a bow at the front. Black stockings, no bra and a bright lipstick.'

I balked at this and he allowed me grey stockings and bronze lipstick.

The Bussys arrived first and we shook hands, Georges Bussy's eyes widening in surprise as he recognised me, but he made no reference to our former acquaintance. He was the sort of twinkly-eyed satyr who could visualize a woman's entire anatomy simply by looking at her ankles, but tonight he was already seeing rather more of me than that. He wore a light grey suit that hid his plump figure but could do nothing about his complexion, while Marguerite looked rather dowdy, I thought, in a flowered dress.

The Hersin-Coupignys showed up soon afterwards, Sylvain in a black suit and black tie under a black overcoat as if going to a funeral, she in an expensive loose *café au lait* creation.

When presented to Hersin-Coupigny he glared sternly at me, and I almost curtseyed. His most prominent feature was a long fleshy underlip that boded ill, so I thought, for the evening ahead.

After an aperitif Serge placed the guests. Normally he allowed me that initiative, and I blinked at him. He put Sylvain on my right and Georges on my left, and sat himself between their wives. I served cold fresh salmon and an elaborate salad with vine leaves as the centre-piece. The table looked inviting: a fine white linen cloth and napkins, copper plates, wafer thin glasses, silver cutlery and a bouquet of tea roses in assorted colours – these a gift from the Bussys.

We had the entrée and a bottle of Sancerre without incident, but when I brought in duck cutlets with mushrooms and carrot puree on toast, Serge remarked that there was nothing to serve with and I extracted myself awkwardly from the table, the men's eyes following me.

Serge was saying: 'Laure-Anne always forgets things.'

This was an absolute lie, apart from being the kind of remark that husbands should keep to themselves in company. 'She's a dizzy baby-doll, usually eats her food with a spoon.' I tossed my head in disgust.

SHC said in a suave nasal voice: 'She's ravishing, she looks almost Cretan. I hope that dress was made in France. These coolie goods will put us all out of work, in no time the Japanese will have us all wandering about in our gardens flying kites for a pastime.' His lower lip glistened at me, and I was not surprised that the town hall secretary went to the police, he would have frightened any girl. I smiled at him and shoved the duck at his wife.

At Serge's request, Georges Bussy was pouring out the Madiran, but my husband told him: 'None for Laure-Anne, one glass of white is enough for her, otherwise she starts getting randy. Highly sensual, she is.' My mouth and eyes opened and he went on: 'Laure-Anne, are you sure this meat is edible? It's like leather.'

Bussy came to my rescue: 'That's because it's real duck, of course.'

SHC chomped away, coming out with sentences between chews: 'I can see that Laure-Anne is a very dutiful wife, I'm sure she knows what's best for us. A wise woman knows her place. Who's that absurd female in the government who wants the masculine and feminine genders deleted from the language?' He pulled a bone from his mouth. 'I think it was a character in George Sand's "Indiana" who said women are vain and imbecile by nature, possessing an idiot credulity provided by The Creator to offset their wily ways. That was the phrase. Yes, they'll always succumb to flattery, he said.'

'Absolutely, *mon vieux*,' his wife retorted. 'But at least we've got something to be flattered about.' She screwed up her nose as Sylvain yanked a scraggy morsel from his teeth and deposited it on the side of his plate.

The damn duck *was* tough, but nobody said anything. As I sawed away daintily at what I can only describe as the *pièce de resistance*, something touched my knee, Hersin-Coupigny's leg. I pulled mine away, only to feel renewed

49

pressure. I rose, fetched more bread, and on resuming my seat was astonished to feel his hand covering my upper leg, then slipping across my tunic into the gulley behind my knees. I coughed and glanced anxiously at him. Forking his food with the other hand, he smiled and nodded at the others who were all talking at once.

I asked SHC for some water and eased myself back in my chair. It was no good; after pouring me the water, his left hand roved about inside my thighs and there was nothing I could do about it. Even so, a minute later I put my hand down, found his cuff and with a demure smile pushed his paw away. He continued molesting me, his hand perilously close to my most intimate part, running a finger along my stocking top through the flimsy cotton of the dress.

'Of course,' Bussy was hooting away, 'since the *Général*, nobody's made the slightest effort to counter the slump. It's the Centrist way, thinking up panic measures week by week. When Chirac takes over in March there'll simply be wholesale privatisation and half our industry will be bought up by foreigners to salvage the situation.'

My assailant withdrew his hand and in carefree style put his arm round my shoulders: 'And are you going to buy some shares, my dear Laure-Anne? What will you do after the election?'

I returned him a look heavy with pathos: 'It's no use asking me, I've never found out what elections are for.' Laughter all round. 'I know we had Civic Instruction at school, but it didn't seem to have any connection with what was happening. Perhaps they've changed it now.'

'Isn't she sweet?' Marguerite said.

Claire put her oar in: 'It's this obsession with market forces and free trade that's at the root of it. We have a system that can't possibly work when nearly half the GDP is paid back in taxes. What has France gained from free trade? There's no such thing as free trade and never has been, because the winners just have to redistribute their wealth. That's ridiculous too, why give money to the poor, they only spend it! We should opt out of the system at once.'

'*Bravo*,' cried the gentleman on my right. 'We must keep out low-wage goods for a start, those people never buy much from us, they're too busy pirating our products.' His hand was under the tablecloth again, touching my belly.

'Perhaps you'd like some more mushrooms, Claire,' I said.

Marguerite complained about the falling dollar, and Sylvain lectured her: 'The Americans have used foreign capital to re-finance their plant, and now their falling currency is designed to boost their exports. They know how to look after themselves. All right! If it's every man for himself, let France do likewise, clear out the old gang and have a government that thinks it through.' When I leant forward to help Claire to mushrooms, my legs parted and he thrust his hand between them. I stood up, and his hand flashed to my bottom under the dress as he added: 'Let the French people consume what the French people produce, not what others dump on us. The Americans are fighting for free trade in armour plating, and we can't let it go on!'

Serge flung an arm into the air royally, to denote that the topic had gone on long enough: 'No indeed. But tell me Sylvain, what do you think of my little wife? She knows how to pick a dress, the neckline is elastic and she can vary the *décolleté*. Show them, *ma biche*, let the gentlemen see your assets.' He seemed half drunk already, and I scowled at him. He glowered back, and he declared: 'She has the finest breasts in Avallon.'

'Really, Serge,' I choked.

'Come, *mon trésor*, we're all friends here. Show them your tits.'

The whole table was cackling except me. Bussy gingerly touched my left sleeve, where upon SHC hauled down the elastic on his side.

'Lovely!' said Claire. 'What a fabulous bosom!'

I made a grab for the men's wrists, but it was useless. Hersin-Coupigny shouted: 'Oh, we must have our money's worth now!' They pulled the dress top down beyond the

51

point of no return, and my breasts spilled out. Quickly adjusting my bodice I ran out amid guffaws.

Serge followed me and seized my arms: 'Don't be a fool, it's only in fun.'

'Then let the others do the clowning. I'm no prude, but this is disgusting.'

'Come back at once, or there'll be hell to pay. They expect you to perform.'

'Perform what? You started this, you planned it. I hate you,' I hissed.

We returned and I meekly took my seat and said I was sorry.

Marguerite patted my hand: 'Don't take any notice. Serge is proud of you and rightly so. How do you manage to keep so firm? No, don't say, that's your secret.'

People started passing me their plates, and I busied myself with the cheese board. The talk veered to new technology. Bussy said: 'Most new technology, like mergers, can be justified at company level, but the result for the nation, and internationally, is a disaster. Who feeds the mounting unemployed? The jobless total is the only parameter that counts in the long term, it brought Lenin and Hitler to power, and today's new technology could bring down the curtain on Western democracy as we know it.'

SHC agreed heartily: 'Thank goodness for that. At least in Germany they got people back to work, they had something to strive for, a 1,000-year vision . . .'

Marguerite exclaimed as I bore in the dessert: 'And here's another vision!' A new bottle of Madiran was uncorked and everyone but me took big gulps. After which Serge added liqueur bottles to the spread, and I asked who wanted coffee. Nobody did.

Hersin-Coupigny's reedy voice urged: 'Do let's see your tits again, Laure-Anne. Be a sport, we can dream about them for weeks.'

'I'd prefer not to,' I said crossly. 'Are you sure nobody wants coffee?'

'The truth is,' Serge said pompously, 'my wife is at heart

an exhibitionist. You should see her parading in front of me sometimes.'

'I'd love to,' Claire said.

'Serge!' I snapped.

'She's a genuine nymphomaniac . . .'

'Really, how interesting,' Claire went on. 'I've never met one socially.'

'I'm not,' I protested, covering my ears.

Serge, flushed and pouring himself a large Calvados, was not to be silenced: 'Permanently on heat. Notice how she keeps her mouth open when she smiles?'

'Serge, whatever's come over you? Even if it were true . . .'

I got no further. There was a chorus of: 'So she *is* one . . . That's proof for you . . . You must be right!'

The men guests had my bodice down again within seconds, and Hersin-Coupigny was openly pawing me. 'Such beauties!' he cried.

I jumped up, but was in a quandary, because if I rushed out again I would be known for ever as a spoilsport by these people – and they would be fearsome adversaries. The whole thing was a horrid plot, my own husband had fixed it, no doubt promising his guests that I was good game for a naughty evening. And now they were all passably drunk. I felt a half-wit standing there with my charlies out, but if I fled I would look an even greater idiot.

'Play with them, make them shake, do a tassle dance,' Bussy roared delightedly.

My shoulders sagged in surrender. If they wanted a show, it might as well be a professional one while I was about it. In the hush that ensued, I suggested huskily to Serge that he put on a cassette of Dave Brubeck's 'Take Five', the super-erotic number in 5/4 tempo which we had used at Les Chabannes on special occasions, notably when I did a belly dance. The rhythmic argument between the music and the dance had never failed to rouse both myself and my public. My reputation was now at stake, and I began rocking my haunches, slowly gliding my hands to my ribs, cupping my full breasts.

'Squeeze harder,' Claire whooped. I wished she would keep quiet.

'Those nipples!' This from SHC.

My strawberries were indeed jutting in supplication, the areolae pink and swollen.

I called out throatily: 'Give me cognac, give me wine!' A glass was offered to my lips and I sipped it langorously. Someone drew my chair clear and I began the dance, feeling rather like the lady in the Bible who did her thing in front of Herod. In my present mood I would have asked for Serge's head on a platter, though he was no John the Baptist!

I finished to a round of applause, and Sylvain suddenly cried out: 'Fifty francs and I'm the first!' He chuckled at his own bravado.

'Fifty from me,' was Bussy's bid.

'And me,' Claire joined in.

The money appeared on the table and Serge yelled: 'Go ahead, there's more where that came from!' I was to understand the significance of the remark later.

Ceremoniously, SHC knelt before me on one knee and pulled me down so that I, too, was kneeling. He advanced his flabby lower lip and took a breast into his mouth, working his jaw like a wine-taster. Then Bussy had his turn on the other breast, reverently lapping and sucking as if he had never seen a pair of tits in his life. After which Claire took over, pawing both breasts with her fingers; her nails dug in and she started giving me nasty little nips on the nipple with her teeth, at which I gave her a sneaky pinch on the arm and she got the message.

I shook them off and I resumed swaying and twirling my hips. Sylvain, I'll give him his due, had a good vocabulary for a business tycoon and now he began to declaim: 'This is how they glorified women in pagan times, when the generative and nutritive organs were held in special reverence. Now alas, they are the subject of shame and scandal thanks to our puritan icoclonasts, sorry iclaco . . . It must be the wine. I mean, thanks to the iconoclasts. Now these parts must be hidden. Thus mankind declines in grace and

54

wisdom, and true sensual living is crushed by narrow ideas and distorted morality. We endure the rule of mediocre degenerates whose leading lights scrupulously conceal their own cowardly crimes, while condemning those who swerve from the path of prudish righteousness. The old-gang governments can lead us all to disaster, famine and war, but woe betide the unlucky fellow who is caught in the wrong bed. What hypocrisy, it makes you vomit!'

The speech was greeted with mingled laughter and applause, out of which came Marguerite's extraordinary enquiry: 'Enjoying it, Laure-Anne?' She really was a little soft in the head; what answer was I expected to give to that?

Serge saved me the trouble as he roared: 'Of course she is, can't get enough of it. Why don't you each take a tit, Sylvain and Georges?' They needed no prompting. 'Afterwards, *chérie*, you can show them how you play with yourself while I'm out at work.'

'That's not true, I do nothing of the sort! Aeeee, stop them Serge, they're driving me frantic!'

The men's mouths were guzzling contentedly at my snow-white breasts, and the effect on me was overwhelming. Nothing now stood in the way of total abandon. I moaned weakly with the pleasure and, because I was leaning forward like a ship's figurehead, I had to steady myself with a hand on the back of a chair. Goodness knows what images were going through the men's minds, perhaps they saw me as some Eternal Mother or Primaeval Great Udder. At last, my rosy-cheeked babies stopped suckling and I thankfully covered my bosom.

But Serge had other ideas. 'Show them what you do,' he repeated, leading me to the centre of the carpet and making me sit with my legs splayed out. By now I was properly dressed and intent on pulling myself together.

'I couldn't, it's too awful of you Serge. You know I . . .'

'Please, please,' the company urged, and Serge hitched up my tunic, guiding my left hand to my crotch before returning to his seat.

Claire cried out: 'Oh, look at those delightful shorts with

the little bow, I really must have some. But Laure-Anne, do take them off, we can't see what you're doing.'

My cheeks were hot from the degradation, and I was loving it! To my sexual arousal there was now added the full flush of the masochist's exquisite suffering. I has lost the battle within myself and I had every intention of going through with this new trial. However I was careful to maintain the pretence of being forced and I shot bashful glances at my impatient audience. This was a necessary part of the act, and I took a long time snaking out of the shorts, ineffectually trying to hide my quim, repeating several times – 'Oh I can't – !'

Everyone's tongue was hanging out by the time they at last got a good look at the object of their salacious interest. Slowly I circled and teased my fingers round my honeypot, spreading open the vaginal lips and glancing vacantly at my five worshippers who gazed in awe at my every movement. The men's cocks must have been bursting through their trousers by now and the women's panties sopping wet from their dilated cunts.

How I relished my harlot's power, knowing that the men were longing to get at me, would have rushed at me like wild beasts had they been alone in the room with me! They were restraining themselves with difficulty, keeping up the civilised veneer, making a bit of a joke out of it all. Ah, how they would have wished it otherwise!

The spectacle was tormenting SHC. Through half-closed eyes I watched him furtively unzipping his tight trousers and heave his shaft and scrotum out over the waistband of his underpants. Expecting him simply to grope himself, I was astonished to see both him and Georges rise and move towards me. My honour as a married woman was now in jeopardy, and I cried out when they loomed over me: 'Serge, Serge! Don't let them touch me. Please Serge, you mustn't let them. I'll fight, yes I will!' I meant what I said, too.

'They won't touch you, I promise.'

Reassured, for his tone seemed determined enough, I eased two fingers into my vaginal canal and speeded up.

Marguerite stood up and hauled her husband back to his seat, but Claire moved next to hers, squatting down with her legs spread and frigged herself under her dress. The royalist bracelets jingled as her arm moved busily beneath the billowing fawn material. Both of us were panting hard. Her features grew ugly and her eyes bulged as she reached a climax with a series of gasps. This brought me to the threshold and I shot my legs forward and screamed, my whole body squirming in a riot of voluptuous sensation that took me out of this world.

I fell back on my elbows just as Hersin-Coupigny's great cock shot a jet of sperm all over my heaving belly. I attempted a smile and closed my eyes.

I was aware of Serge wiping me off with a napkin. The Hersin-Coupignys had evidently mopped themselves up already, for Claire was diligently rubbing the carpet clean next to my feet.

Back at the table everyone gathered round me, embracing and congratulating me, Marguerite twittering: 'My goodness, it was so rude! I've never seen anything like it!'

Shaking, I slumped forward on the table and sought the comfort of my folded arms. Serge offered me solace in the shape of a glass of cognac, murmuring endearments.

'You should have warned me all the same,' I choked.

'One thing led to another.'

'Liar, you planned it all.'

Sylvain was into another speech: 'You know, it really isn't fair, I'm sure women have much more satisfying orgasms than ours . . .' Somebody said it was because we committed 'our whole soul', Georges I think, but I was too flaked out to take part in the debate.

Later when they were all gone I remember Serge staggering about drunkenly trying to put me into a nightdress, and me saying I was too hot.

'I did it for you,' I kept muttering. 'I did it for you.'

By then he was flat on his back snoring.

Chapter Six

It was a surprisingly warm day in early December, a day to alter course, embark on ventures and blow the dust off neglected hopes. This year I would be well ahead with my New Year resolutions!

For years painting had been one of my leisure activities, off and on. It was an occupation that transported me on a magic carpet to a private world safe from self-doubt and anguish, from money worries, ambiguous personal relations, the seven capital sins and the four cardinal virtues. There I could be myself. That crisp December day was the perfect opportunity to begin again a pastime that would provide me with the external challenge my husband had taken such pains to deprive me of. I would tackle him that very evening.

I watched him like a cat waiting for a door to open. I stealthily introduced the subject when he was roaming the living room, passing and re-passing two of my paintings we had agreed to hang, the others being ignominiously stacked against the back wall in the cellar under plastic sheeting.

'Still like them?' I asked airily, indicating the picture of four men teeing up on the golf course at the Evian club-hotel where I originally worked, and the canvas of two little girls from the farm next to Les Chabannes standing on the rungs of a gate overlooking a field.

'They look fine, nice bright colours.' The paintings had no protective glass and once again I felt satisfaction at the yellow-green and russet garb of nature, and the crisp outlines of the crimson and blue figures. But I still wished I could economise further on brushstrokes without veering to cartoon or commercial techniques. My tonal balance needed improvement too.

'I'd like to take it up again.'

'You mean outdoors? All right, we'll take the stuff with us next time we go out for a drive. Might even try a spin later today.'

He was humouring me. I replied: 'It wouldn't be quite the same. How can I put it? You would sort of disturb my particular creative process, because it needs hours at a stretch, and because I love you there would be the emotional influence from outside. You see, sometimes I don't even pick up a brush for half an hour and it can take me an hour to get into the swing, or else I might realise it wasn't my day for some reason. And then when you've been painting for a couple of hours you can't stop.' I added feebly: 'If you see what I mean. You'd be awfully bored perhaps.'

'Hm. It's dangerous going off on your own. Do you realise how many attacks on women there have been in this area alone in the past three months? Sixteen.'

'I'd be careful, keep a look-out. And it wouldn't cost anything much, I'd pay for it myself.'

'Can't you paint here in the flat? From postcards? Yes, that's a good idea.'

'No, postcards are fine for practising, but . . .' I could not go on, there was no point in explaining, he did not understand, and we would be off on another argument about woman's role, which wasn't the issue at all. I wanted to cry.

He shrugged: 'Perhaps you're right. But we can't have you running around the countryside with nobody knowing where you are, we'll talk about it some other time. Now, if you don't mind, I must phone the office.'

I disappeared into the bedroom and stood with clenched

fists, riding out the anger and sense of injustice. This time however, I was determined to defy him, the issue was too important. I had gladly become his slave in every other department of our life together, but now he was snatching from me the one thing I had always been able to fall back on. There could be no compromise, I was free to resist as well as to submit. My brain whirled through a vaguely-perceived list of frustrated geniuses who had triumphed over a Philistine environment. I would dig my heels in. I had the brains to see this through, in fact my I.Q. was measured at well over 130. I mentioned this once to Serge, and he demanded to know who measured me; I unwisely quipped that the rating was worked out by computer in a Champs-Elysées shopping arcade, and the discussion ended there!

The good weather held. I still had the use of my car, which Serge had been too busy to put up for sale. I checked over what canvases, paints, chemicals and brushes I possessed, then squandered 600 francs in a hardware shop on new items including a 150 francs canvas and two others costing about 100 each. The next day I drove in a generally westward direction until I spotted a quaint old shop in a hamlet called Vieille Eglise. On that occasion I stayed only a couple of hours sketching the outline of a painting, and then returned leaving the materials, including my venerable fold-up easel, in the car boot.

Other excursions followed, before disaster struck on the fourth sortie. On that still-warm day, at around 4 p.m., I paused in my labours and leaned back on my stool against the ivy-covered wall opposite the old shop. I gazed fondly at the easel and cleared my mind of thought. I was pleased with my work, the birds twittered, chickens clucked and a tractor moaned its way across a distant field. Removing my pinafore, thick with paint of every imaginable shade, I donned my coat, tipped my beret on the back of my head and relaxed.

– to wake shivering at close on 6 p.m.! In the dark! There was a sour taste in my mouth and panic in my breast, for Serge was due home at 6.30 p.m.!

I made la rue du Chateau with five minutes to spare, charging into the apartment, meaning to clean my hands and get something going for dinner.

There in the living-room reading the post was Serge. Only one word was appropriate, and I used it between clenched teeth before facing him.

'Oh, you're home already,' I observed brightly. 'I went for a drive.'

'Yes, nothing much doing so I . . .' He broke off, took one look at my multi-coloured fingers, narrowed his eyes and stated: 'Painting! You've been painting!'

'Yes, I thought I might . . .'

'Let's inspect the result, then. Where's your tackle?'

'Um, in the car. I'll go and fetch what I've done.'

'I'll come down with you, it's simpler.'

And there in the boot was the full array of evidence. A couple of virgin canvases, tubes of paint that had never been squeezed in their lives, half a dozen brushes with shiny new wine-coloured handles, and on the third canvas the drying paint from my sessions at the village shop. There was nothing to be said, and neither of us spoke. Serge stared at me coldly, undisguised lust in his eyes.

Upstairs I cleaned my hands with scouring powder, soap and white spirit, served the master his drink and busied myself out of his reach. All without a word between us.

I was gutting a couple of trout when he ordered: 'Come here.' he announced, I went in, to the living-room, still clad in the old brown skirt and mustard blouse I had been wearing all day.

'For your punishment you will serve my meals for the next three days wearing only a black belt, black stockings and black high-heeled shoes. Change at once, and I want you to apply lipstick to your nipples.'

I got into the specified garb, and he ordered: 'Go to the toolbox and bring me the length of electric wire coiled up there.' This I did, keeping in the shadows, because the lights were on. 'Now stand over here so that I can see you.'

'Let's draw the curtains,' I pleaded. 'Everyone will see!

61

There are some people in the flats, a man at the window and he's looking this way.'

'Let him look.'

'Please Serge, no electricity, it's against the law, I could have a heart attack!'

'Pull the belt tighter. That's nice, emphasises your bottom, and it's about time it felt the sting of chastisement again. How long is it since the last time?'

'I don't know, I've been so good,' I cried.

'Yes, there's not a blemish on them, not the suspicion of a stripe. Now touch your toes. How many this time?'

'I don't know Serge, I've been *very* good.'

'Four, I think, as I'm using wire and it will hurt.'

'Yes, four is enough.'

'Please?'

'Please. I mean, *please* Serge.'

He gripped my neck and forced me to bend over more. I kept my eyes closed tight as the wire hit my behind four times in quick succession. The lashes cut my bare skin terribly hard, but it was all too fast for me to cry out, and there were no extras this time.

'You're getting plumper. Now stand up. What do you say?'

'Thank you Serge.'

I rubbed my smarting flesh, my breath hissing between my teeth; it was true. I did seem chubbier, curving out like a pair of beach balls. Serge spun me round and touched my fleece: 'What a mess, the slightest thing makes you wet down there.'

'Serge, the curtains!'

He consented to close them, but eventually it was in this awful condition that I was obliged to produce the meal, lay the table and eat with him.

As ordered, I greeted him similarly dressed the next evening, when he thought up something even worse than whipping me.

We had begun the main dish, a steak and kidney pudding, when his knife and fork clattered onto his plate. I felt the blood drain from my face.

'*Qu'est que c'est que cette saloperie?*' he cried in a high-pitched disbelieving tone.

'I beg your pardon,' I replied primly.

'Taste it.' I had to admit there was something odd about it. 'What's it supposed to be?'

'Er, the meat's a little hard. It said three hours, but I didn't expect you so early.'

'The pastry's too thick, it tastes like an old car tyre!' He was yowling away an octave too high.

He rose, took my arm and strode into the bedroom, with me stumbling along behind. He selected a trouser hanger, one of those things with two slats of felt-covered wood held tight by a metal device. He tried the hanger on his little finger, then to my horror told me to push my breasts together.

Retreating from him, I cried: 'Oh no, you'll squash them, it's dangerous, you'll injure me!'

He flicked the mechanism into place and I let out an almighty shriek that must have been heard all over the building and left me panting, with my mouth wide open. He let the hanger go and it hung down, tugging at my poor nipples. He led me back to the table and I held the hanger up as I walked. It was torture, deliberate torture, and I told him so, but he pushed my plateful of meat pudding closer and fitted my fingers round a spoon. In this ridiculous and excruciatingly painful state, one hand holding up the hanger, I had to finish my food, gulping the pudding down with difficulty and sobbing like a little girl so that I could hardly see the stuff.

'Hurry up, Laure-Anne, there's a good girl, and let this be a lesson,' he said, as if he were my father.

'Yes, Serge,' I cried, the gluey substance distorting my words. I pleaded: 'Please take it off, I know you're not really cruel.' (Not much, the sod!). 'I've finished it.'

He grinned: 'You know you love this, *ma petite*. And you know I've got a big hard-on looking at you.'

'I'm glad, S-Serge. Now may I take it off?'

He gave a nod and I removed the appliance, to find my nipples flat and frighteningly elongated. Blood rushed into

63

them and I cupped my hands over myself to ease the burning.

My 'daddy' then commanded me to crouch under the table, where I helped him draw down his trousers, and fell to kissing his iron-hard rod. He came quickly and I swallowed his seed. That was my only dessert that evening.

A little later he stood at the kitchen doorway watching my naked bottom as I bent down to fill the dishwasher.

If this account is starting to read along the lines of *Les Misérables*, I must hasten to balance my story. For the scenes of degradation were only an occasional part of our life together. We had good times, too, in the conventional sense.

Increasingly, as I now realise, I interacted with my husband, provoking the indignities he inflicted upon me. My pulse would quicken the instant I knew that he was going to lecture me or punish me, and this would set off the familiar thrill in my neck, chest and stomach. At those moments I truly wanted him to order me about and craved the assurance that he desired me and relied on me alone for his special kind of pleasures. I knew I counted, knew he would protect me and look after me, come what may, because he had no choice either.

The excitement I enjoyed could, I suppose, be compared with the thrill some women feel when they shoplift, it is a yearning for attention in another outlandish way. Although I personally have never stolen so much as a packet of sweets in my life, I have read that it's the 'being naughty' that inspires a woman filching things from a store, be she a duchess or a working man's wife; and that she really wishes to be punished for the dreadful thing she has done, this punishment for sin being proof that Society is not ignoring her. At the same time, some experts suggest, she is trying to escape into childhood because the grown-up world is too awful to deal with, too complicated. Similarly I basked in the power I had to provoke Serge's wish to hurt me, and at the same time his authoritarian behaviour reassured me.

I was a little girl again! Thus Serge and I were locked in a passionate saga of wrongdoing and penance.

There was some light relief, however. We laughed together and had fun like anyone else. To cite one small example, our scornful comments on the TV news were remarkably similar, in a way they were a sign of compatibility in this electronic age. In bed I loved snuggling up to him, receiving his kisses both tender and ardent as we fondled each others' hair and faces after lovemaking. I loved to lie with my quim jammed against his muscled left thigh and liked sneaking my fingers with infinite care to his penis in the early hours and gently rousing it so that it grew from a soft wormy thing to a straining length of thick stiff flesh, and he would grunt and instinctively spread his legs thus giving me full access to his balls, and if he stirred too much I would craftily snake my hand away and he would turn naturally towards me in his sleep and I would hug myself with joy in the dark.

Let me reminisce, too, about the unforgettable evening we spent during our first winter. I had the log fire going and the tablecloth spread on the carpet and laid out with a kind of fireside buffet. When Serge came in his surprise was a joy to see, and he whirled me round and slipped willingly into the mood. He changed into a pair of thin jogging shorts and I wore my honeymoon wrap. We tucked into hot salmon cutlets, a Russian salad and fruit cake with cream, the whole feast washed down with a Gamay. To help the romantic mood, he played a cassette of Latin American music, and when the first side was over he replaced it with the Bach D minor concerto for two violins, surely one of the eternal masterpieces. At that moment I knew he wanted to please me and woo me.

'*Je t'aime, me chérie,*' he said simply, pushing the plates aside to give us space on the cloth, 'and it's a little deeper every day. I can't do without you now.'

'Don't add a word to that, *mon prince*. I've never been happier either.'

'After the life I lead you?'

'Have I ever complained?'

65

'Often, but I disregard it.'

We snuggled up, gradually flowing into the preliminaries of love-making. Sascha Gawriloff and Friedrich Wührer played as equal partners, and so did we, both of us performing with technical brilliance, exchanging dulcet courtesies, avowing our enjoyment of each other, and expressing our mutual esteem in time with the music. As the matchless largo began, I lay back blissfully to receive my lover's homage, and the slow majestic fugue brought us to an ecstasy that we had never achieved until then. Thus we mingled our souls and the Hamburg Chamber Orchestra under Walter Goehr would certainly have been proud of us.

As the concerto drew to a close I whispered: 'Serge, *mon adoré pour toujours*, I would love us to have a baby, two babies. Let's have a girl next year and then a boy. I want to give you babies, so that we can see ourselves live in our children.'

'And what about the house?'

'Why not? We can have that too, we can afford it. France needs children, the posters say so. We are healthy and babies would complete our happiness, we'd be so proud of them.'

He poured out the rest of the Gamay: 'It's a major programme, my broody little hen.'

'We're big enough to carry it through. It would be such fun, a lovely house and toddlers and lots of interesting friends and barbecue parties and everything. We would be spreading happiness and light, we're so lucky – it's our duty!'

His eyes stared at the ceiling: 'Let me mull it over, we blokes take a while to get accustomed to these things. Now, if you'll excuse me, I must pay a call in the bathroom.'

'No,' I said, 'let's make love again first, you'll find it's much better when you're like that.' He trusted me, and said afterwards that it was fantastic for him.

Even so, Serge worries me. He could switch from being a normal everyday chap to acting like a fiend possessed by

66

drink or drugs or both. After all, he had once been in the Brigade des Stupéfiants er du Proxénetisme (BSP) and a suspicion about drugs kept nagging at me. He had the know-how.

I paid an unannounced morning visit to Les Chabannes. I was unsure what I would find and my reasons were various. Nostalgia for the old place and its routine was part of it – I was sorry that I had been ignoring my friends – in addition I was curious to know how the club was doing under the new management.

Little had changed. I strolled in casually after parking my Lada, admiring the familiar ochre and red buildings on the way, noticing the lavender sign in the hall which read 'Les Chabannes – Reception' and rediscovering the gratifying country hotel atmosphere.

I stood quietly in the hall for a few moments before I saw anyone. Somebody was shifting a bed upstairs, someone else was stacking plates in the kitchen. This had been home for me not a year previously, and 51% of it had been mine. I had been 'Mademoiselle', supervising everything, busy with the accounts most days, touting for business, wangling every conceivable favour from Ministers, officials and magnates. Among members I recalled Thernissier of the Quai d'Orsay, Madame Chavaux who was the *eminence grise* among women politicians and preferred our nubile popsies to her husband, Souchaud of the Elysée Palace who would phone me when his buddy the West German Bundesminister required my services during a visit to Paris, Picard who was a possible for the French Presidency itself. So many ghosts from the past. For a moment it occurred to me to throw out a challenge to Serge, namely, that he give me my freedom to do my own thing, or I would return to Les Chabannes and satisfy my entrepreneurial itch among the nation's upper crust.

Véronique clomped down the stairs and caught sight of me: 'Laure-Anne! How wonderful!!!!' She ran the last few steps and we embraced. Then a whole bevy emerged from nowhere: Solange, Bernadette, Mauricette and of course Blandine.

'*Mes enfants*,' I burst out.

'How's married life?' someone said.

'If only you knew!' I cried, apropos of nothing.

'Drinks all round,' Blandine ordered.

'We can't drink the profits!' I protested.

'They may be the last we have,' she laughed. 'Anyhow, who cares, I'm the boss now. Champagne, Benoit!'

Véronique, a ravishing dark-haired beauty whom I had personally recruited, hauled me over to the bar: 'Are you pregnant?'

'Well, not quite.' Howls of laughter as the flute glasses were lined up.

'Have you dropped in for a quickie?' said Bernadette. 'Is he impotent or something like that?' Now well over 30 and still an adolescent at heart, Bernadette dated from my Top Club days. She said: 'What's it like with the same man all the time? It must be pretty boring.'

'I make sure it's not. You've put on weight, Bernadette.'

'Oh the cow! As a matter of fact, fatties are back in vogue, we have entered the age of the belly.' Giggles.

'She won't admit she's got herself in the family way,' Solange drawled.

Mauricette handed round the glasses: 'Tell me, do you beat him up?' She was a vicious sadist, much in demand by gentlemen who were prepared to drop their trousers and receive her lashes.

'No, he whips me, but I make him pay for it. Here's health!'

Blandine growled: 'Don't talk about health, we're all scared out of our wits with this AIDS commotion. You're well out of it, Laure-Anne, we are a dying industry like steel and textiles. Talk about the wrath of God! We're almost living like nuns, the members are so goodie-goodie. They bring their wives in droves, we're really bourgeois these days.'

Véronique giggled: 'It's like that book "1984" where everyone stopped having sex. Maybe it's happened already, how very frustrating.' More giggles, with wisecracks at every turn, some passable and others feeble.

Blandine and I took a turn in the grounds, swapping tales from the past. I kept glancing at the house and the big barn, for I had been serious with Serge about buying a house. I could see it in my mind's eye, topping a hillock overlooking woodland, a long and low structure with Mediterranean arches, the sun streaming into the L-shaped lounge through wisteria-decked windows, and with sweet-smelling bedrooms. Outside there would be a lush lawn and flower-flanked paths and a swing for the children along with a little log cabin. A pony would graze in a small enclosure.

'You're looking peaky,' said my companion with an inquisitive look. 'Sort of anguished.'

'Nonsense, I'm excited to see you all, that's all. And after all, we are in mid-winter despite the fine day.'

'How's Serge turning out? I mean, are you happy?'

'Gloriously. He says I deserve a long rest, so I'm just lazing around. I do some painting though.' I told a whole lot more fibs, and we went in.

The visit left me sad, especially at having to tell lies. It ought not to be necessary a few months after getting married. Why was it happening?

I was even more crestfallen when Serge informed me he had found a customer for my Lada, none other then the widow Liliane. She was hiding round too many corners for my liking. What was happening there?

Yes indeed, Serge worried me. Maybe he was one of those schizophrenic cases . . .

Chapter Seven

A yell shot out from the bathroom a few days before Christmas 1985. Serge was taking a shower.

'Whatever happened?' I cried, rushing in.

'The soap fell down.'

'Eh?'

'The soap fell and hit me on the foot.'

'Ah,' I said. 'There's nothing much I can do about that.'

'Why can't we have rounded soap like they have in the ads, instead of soap with corners?'

'Square soap is cheaper, and as you've imposed an austerity campaign we have square soap. Next time you can go shopping for your own. Only don't start hitting some poor innocent woman while you're there.'

'Ha-ha. Hit a woman – me?'

'Yes, you nearly did last Saturday. There was that unfortunate old lady dithering about – your phrase – and you said, "Watch out madam, you'll get hurt if you don't make a decision" and she said, "What?" and you said, "Someone could hit you and it might be me." That's what you said.'

'Ha-ha-ha. At last, someone gave her something to think about for a few days. Listen, *bijou*, you're invited to our dinner on Christmas Eve at that restaurant next to the Commissariat, as I'm on duty.'

'Oh, that's wonderful!'

'It'll be a simple meal, so that our families and friends can cheer us up. Nothing elaborate.'

Leaning against the door jamb, I gazed dreamily at his naked body: 'Isn't it marvellous being husband and wife, a real live couple. I still can't believe it.' He cocked his head, finding no suitable comment, and turned the shower back on.

There were about a dozen of us at the dinner, and I was quietly proud to be consoling the bulls for being on duty. No women staff worked on that day, but the Commissaire, the boss lady, looked in for a drink. There seemed nothing special about her, and naturally she was in mufti that night, but she looked competent, and must have been so to be put in charge of the men. I liked the idea that I was becoming part of this special community, and the *esprit de corps* was tangible. Also part of the close-knit community was Liliane, wearing a slinky green outfit. Everyone strove to cheer her up while taking care not to overdo it. Nevertheless she shed a few tears around 11 p.m. as the Muscadet and Cahors took effect. People had to pop out occasionally as duty called, but we got through a salver or two of seafood, some sweetmeats, white pudding, pheasant, salad, charlotte and other desserts. At midnight we opened the champagne and the bereaved Liliane ended up with her copper tresses on Serge's neck.

Bubbly also flowed on the night of December 31, which provided the first warning that something might be wrong with my health. The venue was the Bazillac flat and we thought we had to accept because we had never formally exchanged invitations.

As usual I drank little, and yet after the New Year toast I sank onto the settee, wanting nothing so much as my own soft pillow. It was odd. From beneath heavy eyelids I observed and listened to the others.

Claire Hersin-Coupigny was banging on about free trade again: 'In the past decade we have slipped back half a century or more. What nobody tells you is that none of the trade crises has ever been solved, they have simply been interrupted by war. This is no longer possible with today's mass weapons of destruction.'

It was the usual disjointed party talk with nobody really listening to anyone else. Joe, one of three single men of about 40, declared: 'So we are left with crime and speculation. Hence the black economy, which is keeping the whole system going. The facade is cracking, the smoke-screen of fear and greed is hiding something very dangerous – the fetid odour of decadence. Ours is a system creating the greatest misery for the greatest number, as Arthur Miller said long ago.'

Hubert our host corrected him: 'Oh, come on, he was referring to the United States. All right then, if war is out, where do we go from here?'

Joe replied like a shot: 'Economic collapse. Peace is now the greatest threat to the West; this new fellow Gorbachev has only to withdraw the Soviet menace and the US ballgame is finished.'

Hersin-Coupigny cut in: 'It's dangerous, I agree. No policies mean no votes. We had that before when half the electorate stayed away from the polls.'

He gave the impression that that ought to have been the last word, but Liliane sidled up: 'If they can only push my shares up I'll be happy, I always vote better on a rising market!'

Hubert ventured: 'What they're trying to do is ensure that at least two-thirds of the voters are better off, however many people are marching in the streets.'

At that point I dozed off and began to dream. I was a little girl again, back home in our drawing-room in the Paris suburbs. Everyone swaying about above me. I was frightened and wanted to escape the crush but a huge figure loomed over me and I could not move. In fact it was Gaston, one of Joe's friends, asking me to dance. Gaston steered me over to the bar where I had some orange juice and we swanned into the general melee to some 1940's melody.

Snippets of talk reached me. Jacques, the third unac-companied man, was saying: 'I don't even agree with the laws of physics, let alone any so-called divine laws; only this week I dropped a priceless old copy of Les Contes de Perrault as I was taking it off the shelf, and it's ruined. What purpose did the law of gravity serve in that case? It could have been suspended, nobody was looking. Ha-ha-ha!'

Diane said, incomprehensibly, to me, 'Anyhow, the devil seems much more friendly than the divinity!'

I caught sight of Joe holding hands with Hubert, Sylvain was sitting against a wall beside an 18-year-old girl with his hand up her skirt, Claire was dancing with another young girl and their bellies rocked as one, Diane glided around with Jacques. Serge and Liliane were nowhere to be seen.

Claire's dancing partner remarked: '. . . Of course I've only his word for it, and even if it's true nobody's going to tell her, she doesn't suspect a thing . . .'

In a valiant attempt to pull myself together and show an interest I enquired: 'Who doesn't suspect what? Do let me in on the scandal.'

The girl blushed and pretended to sneeze, by which time we had drifted apart.

It was stifling hot, I felt faint and had difficulty focusing my eyes. Judging from the general behaviour, we seemed to be heading for an orgy, and the prospect filled me with dread. Already my partner was fondling my bottom and trying to make me. Sad at heart, I searched more systematically for my husband, as Gaston and I glided into the passage and then into the unlighted bedroom.

Gaston told me: 'You're a lovely girl, do you want it?' His hand wandered to my V-neck. Why oh why did everyone think I was easy prey?

'Sorry, I've an appointment for the night. Thank you for the compliment, you're not bad yourself . . .' That was the last I remembered, for I must have slumped against him and passed out. Instinct brought me to my senses, and I found myself spread-eagled on the guests' coats with Gaston trying to tear off my panties.

'W-what's going on?' I mumbled. The fellow clamped a heavy hand over my mouth. Rolling and kicking out weakly I hit a small table lamp that crashed to the floor. We both froze, and then, miraculously, Serge was there, with his hand on the main light switch. He grabbed Gaston by the scruff of the neck and hauled him from the room with his trousers and underpants round his shins.

Diane entered and we staggered into the bathroom. Breathing out drink fumes she locked the door and stood with my panties in her hand. I sat on the edge of the bath and announced: 'I'm going to be sick.'

'You've had too much, *ma chérie*.'

'No, there was something in the drink.'

She sort of snarled: 'You said you'd come again and see me, but you didn't.'

I tottered to the door: 'I must have air, I can't breath.'

Serge bundled me across the landing into our flat where he opened the window wide and I stood gulping in the heavenly cool air.

'What was all that about?' he said sternly.

'Goodness knows, Serge. I'm ill, I feel so ill, I need a doctor, there's something the matter with me.'

'What happened in the bedroom?'

'I don't know, I honestly don't, I just passed out. Thank goodness you arrived. Where were you? Where was Liliane?'

'We went out for a stroll.'

'And a fuck! You came in here, you used our flat!'

He took an arm gently: 'You don't know what you're saying. Bed for you.'

I sank into his arms: 'Put me to bed, I do love you, I feel better already. I wish we'd never gone to their dreadful party.' I yawned. 'I'll be all right, let me wash my mouth out and you can give me a big kiss for 1986. What is your duty tomorrow?'

'I've got a day off. We won't set the alarm.'

Minutes later Serge had a pillow under my middle and was driving his cock into my inert body, while my head was crooked at 30°, thumping repeatedly against the wooden bedhead. I was helpless, looking down at our two pelvises heaving up and down.

My last thought before I passed out was that at least he was not poking Liliane!

A few days later I passed out again. Here is how it happened.

On two successive occasions during that January, Serge was unable to make love. For the second time my stallion's tackle hung limp as a harness on a nail, and he took the misfortune badly. But handling this type of male setback had emerged as one of my specialities over the years, and I set to work.

'Maybe it's too much celebrating, or the 'flu wave, or maybe it's Halley's comet,' I grinned.

'It's never happened before.'

'But it will again, and there's nothing to worry about. You need some new fantasies. Imagine I'm Marilyn or Liliane.'

'Liliane?'

'Gish,' I supplied hastily. 'Tell me when you first jerked off as a boy, was it sliding down a rope at school? Or did it happen on a scout rally?'

'Are you trying to be funny?'

'I know what I'm doing,' I scolded. 'It's all in your mind, and anyhow we women are so curious.'

He countered: 'Since this is your idea, you tell first.'

I told him how I had my first weeny orgasm around the age of 11 when I was in my room doing homework and listening to an Elvis Presley number on the radio. How I began swaying and went 'all-velvet' and later found a damp patch on the cushion. I concluded: 'I soon got the hang of it, and wanked myself day and night for weeks. Ah, the innocence of childhood!'

He sniffed, gave an embarrassed cough and began: 'In my case it was by accident.'

'It usually is.' I tucked my hand in his and gazed up at him in adoration. He had lost his self-assurance and I was determined he should have it back.

He coughed again: 'We had this friend of my mother's in one Sunday, and I was being shown off, aged about 13.

The woman was dolled up in one of those tight black suits, she was youngish and had glossy lips and nail varnish and a pillbox hat with a veil. Her knees showed and she fiddled with her skirt and crossed her legs this way and that all the time. I couldn't keep my eyes off her stockings.'

'That's why she kept crossing her legs.'

'She wore tight gloves too and the room was thick with the smell of her perfume. I can remember it even now. She repeatedly said she wouldn't stay long and that made me anxious. Anyhow, I felt my prick going stiff and it hurt against my jeans and I didn't know what was happening to me. Then later in bed I got it hard again and the inevitable happened.'

'Ooh,' I said enthusiastically. 'Did you see it shoot out? Your stuff, I mean?'

'Not that time.'

In consequence of which, I fixed myself up with a tight-fitting black suit, pillbox hat, gloves and the rest as per his description, and we acted out the childhood scene in the living room, with Serge doing to me on the carpet what he had secretly lusted to do to that woman for a quarter of a century.

The close-fitting suit was killing me however, and afterwards I lay for ten minutes in a daze, my heart pounding. Serge said I looked like a ghost.

I was ordered to the doctor and had a blood test. The verdict was – severe anaemia.

I blamed Serge openly, telling him it would never have happened if I had had a proper job to interest me. He stubbornly refused to admit this, but announced that we were off to the Côte d'Azur, more precisely to Antibes, in late February.

The trip seemed a long time materialising, and the anaemia was wearing me down. I was more than willing for Serge to be the master of my fate, but not to be beaten by some underhand bug of deficiency. Whatever they say, most women like being ill, it seems to me, but health problems annoy me as much as the idea of death itself. It should not be allowed – we should all be as immortal as gods.

So I would stand at the bedroom window for ten minutes at a time, gawping at the rain bouncing off the roofs in tiny particles, or listening to it tinkling down the drainpipes. Every chimney pot for 200 metres around was familiar to me, and so was a green flashing sign in the distance that accorded five seconds' display of Thomson, Philips, Sony and Kenwood in turn, then showed an arrow that blinked for another five seconds, finally producing a galaxy of stars at two bleeps a second for another five seconds. Oh yes, I knew that sign to the ultimate millisecond and was torn between fascination and a crazy desire to creep out with the bread knife and slash the cable. I felt as green as the sign and more than once simply skipped even the small snack I was supposed to have when Serge was out all day or all night.

The nadir of my existence occurred, I think, one afternoon when a man somewhere in the building banged in nails for three hours without stopping: eight small taps and a bang, then a tiddly tap for luck – over and over and over. I began to wonder whether I had leukaemia or Diane had given me what was now being described as the most serious world plague for five centuries, and whether Serge and the doctors were in a conspiracy of silence. I could put my mind to nothing, and would lay prostrate for hours, or else stand behind the lounge curtains watching a woman opposite bring up her baby's wind.

However, one evening Serge and I moved from the dinner table into the bedroom with the enthusiasm of new-lyweds, and I was overjoyed to think I might be emerging from the gloom. As bad luck would have it, while just beginning to get ourselves worked up, the doorbell rang.

Serge peeped through the spyhole, waving at me to join him. 'Two women, fat and thin,' he whispered.

In turn I looked through and then glanced back at him: 'Jehovah's Witnesses. I once bought a book and they keep coming back. Want them to join us?'

The bell rang again and Serge, still naked, opened the

door. The fat lady stuttered: 'S-sorry Monsieur, W-we'll come back another time.'

'You'd better not,' he snapped, 'or I'll cut your fingers off and you'll bleed to death.' I thumped him on the arm.

Curiously, I never saw them doing their rounds again; we had driven them out of town, and Serge said they were probably scared of the fire and brimstone.

The incident gave us our first real laugh together for weeks.

Chapter Eight

For generations the Côte d'Azur has been a mecca for the rich and powerful. It is the home of the international jet set and a showcase for the kind of lifestyle that most of us yearn for but can only dream of. We see it on the television, in the movies – and in the adverts. It represents the ultimate in luxury. In short, here is the good life.

It would be an exaggeration to say that Jean-Marc and Aline Blin were the very *crème de la crème* of the Côte but they had certainly raised the good life to the level of perfection. The Côte was their home, they were its local inhabitants. They at least were safe and gave assurance to the well-heeled visitor from northern industrial Europe, from the cyclones and dustbowls of the United States, the swelter of Latin America, the parched soil of Africa and the suspect smells of Asia. They had settled where a golden sun shines most of the time on a cobalt sea.

Their *fin de siècle* terracotta villa inland from Antibes and the Baie des Anges spoke for their discerning taste. Their alert expressions told you they were enjoying every last grain of life's bounty, to the extent that you felt the urge to tell them how glad you were to be with them, to bask in their happiness.

They had a pair of navy blue Lancia cars, a maid and gardener, a couple of black Rottweiler guard dogs and a swimming pool. They had made a success of living, it was something in their souls. I was not alone in my envy of their lifestyle, that was certain. Of more immediate importance, my lethargy seemed to slip away after five minutes in their company.

Jean-Marc, who according to Serge ran an estate agency as a front for his own property ventures, enjoyed a catalogue of delights ranging from 'unforgettable' encounters and 'unrivalled' events along the Côte to 'incredibly lucky' deals and the 'long-awaited rapture' of acquiring a valuable painting for a song. His serene *joie de vivre* masked an undoubted business acumen that had left a few well-placed lines on his chubby face. Aline, for whom Serge had performed a good turn some years earlier during a robbery investigation, was a tall redhead who wore her hair swept to one side. Most of her clothes came from San Remo in Italy and were quietly 'exquisite' – an adjective she included in every other sentence. She owned apartments in Antibes and handled all the accounts, dismissing money as of no importance, which was undoubtedly true in her case. She had the knack of making me feel I was as gorgeous and elegant as herself.

Declining their kind invitation to stay with them, we booked in at *Le Royal* and lunched with them at *Le Dauphin* before driving to their villa. That evening we were due at an unknown destination, unknown solely to me, that is.

'It's not fair,' I protested. Jean-Marc had promised it would be 'the night and day of your life', and I had no choice but to play along with their mysterious game.

At 9 p.m. we reached the night club somewhere near the Antibes yacht harbour and swept under a sign which read *Jimmy's* in blue lettering and past a pair of bouncers. Our coats were whisked away and a lackey in a shiny blue jacket, cream trousers and a pink bow tie led us under an array of spotlights – placed presumably so that everyone could inspect newcomers – into an area where three ranks of tables bordered a round dance floor.

I gripped Serge's arm and endeavoured to look devastating. He had told me to pack my low-cut strawberry dress of mid-thigh length; I had argued that this was hardly appropriate for February but he had overruled me. Aline, too, wore a dress above the knees, in eau-de-nil. Both men wore dark suits with bright ties, and we must have looked like two Union Corse couples as we settled into our table in the middle row and were obsequiously served a house cocktail. Our hosts waved to some acquaintances and Jean-Marc exchanged pleasantries with the waiter. My eyes became used to the low lighting, and noted that there must have been about 50 people in the club, although others were arriving. On each table stood a silver candlestick with a lilac candle that shone onto what appeared to be a primrose cloth, it was hard to tell.

'At least we shall be able to read the menu,' I said brightly. I was wrong.

'There's no menu, actually,' Aline said. 'They bring everything and we eat what we like, much less fuss, and after all we're here for the show. We *are* allowed to choose the wine, however.' This last option was dealt with and we sat back to watch a few couples tangoing on the dance floor.

We joined them, swapping husbands, and I asked Jean-Marc: 'Come on now, what's the secret? This is a club like any other. I've been in the business, why talk about staying a night and a day?'

'This is only the first part. You'll see, if the weather holds.' Yielding to my questions he finally admitted that a yacht trip was planned.

Later, as we had our oysters, a seven-piece band discreetly took their places. A glass ball descended from the ceiling, rotating slowly, its mirrored facets casting furtive colours over us all.

Then there was a drum roll and a brief fanfare. Light flooded the central space and a line of six girls with orange frills round their waists marched around to a military tune, showing off their bare breasts. They had long hair and top hats and sported garters, while a triangle of material between their legs cleverly emphasised their mounds and was thin enough also to catch in their slits. As we admired the girls' powdered bottoms a bitter-sweet nostalgia for Les Chabannes left me silent.

The artists twirled, waved their top hats, performed little jumps that made their breasts bounce, waggled their legs this way and that and, finally bent downward and touched their toes, arranging themselves at intervals so that everyone in the audience was faced with at least one big peach of an arse. A classic debut.

The *animateur* pranced in, a stocky bald man in a silver monkey suit who began auctioning each girl in turn to the gentlemen. A hefty American bawled out: 'If you take Diner's Club, I'll take two for 1,000 dollars. Pack 'em up right away.' He looked pleased with his quip, and it raised a small laugh. But payment was cash on the nail and the winners had to fetch the girl and take her back to their table. One diner acted the clown, pretending his wife was holding him back. Another actually tripped and ended up on the floor. This horsing around got the evening going and we had a real comic after that, followed by a conjuror.

It so happens that I cannot abide conjurors, and I looked about me to see how the showgirls were faring. One had a boob hard up against her fellow's mouth, another was roughing her customer's hair as he explored the inside her triangle, a couple of garters were being held aloft, one eventually came flying through the air to sail over the conjuror's head. Jean-Marc laid a hand on my thigh and asked if I liked the show and I could only reply that it was super. He kept his hand there during the next turn, some men dancing in loincloths with nothing on underneath – correction – with flesh-coloured G-strings on underneath. We ordered another bottle and I felt Jean-Marc's hand sneaking into my *entre jambe* and I pushed it away, adding the single word 'no' with a smile.

The silver master of ceremonies quietened the applause as the conjuror made his exit: 'Now Mesdames-Messieurs, we come to the climax! The doors are closed, we are all friends together, but kindly refrain from all comment during this item. The girl you will see is a bone fide stranger whom we – er – acquired in a Scandinavian country. She is an unwilling participant, I must stress, and we are sure you will enjoy her – er – performance. *Merci*.' We were so cowed nobody applauded.

The room went pitch black except for the candles on the tables, and there was a good deal of bumping and rumbling. From the loudspeakers came a low rhythmic thrumming, then subdued red lighting came from floor level and an outsize candle flickered into life on the set. This large candle, black in colour, stood on an altar and next to it were gold or brass ornaments: stars, orbs, an inverted cross. The figure 666 was embroidered on the altar cloth, clouds of incense that came from a censer and floated above the floor lighting.

What purported to follow was, of course, a Black Mass. But I cannot say whether it was authentic, being unwilling to ask the others and thus erroneously indicate that I was interested. Satanism is frankly not my idea of fun, but presumably the believers in the audience appreciated the charade or it would not have been staged. Several women looked on with parted lips as a bunch of 'clergy' stood round the altar chanting what Aline told me were real prayers backwards. A fair-haired girl of about 18 was brought in struggling between a pair of muscular men dressed like executioners. The girl wore an ordinary flowered skirt and a white blouse, to 'prove' that she really had been kidnapped. A priest blindfolded her and, with extravagant arm-waving, the celebrants removed her clothes and rubbed something over her lips, ears, nipples and navel.

Aline gave me an extraneous snippet: 'I'm told the Opus Dei men go in for mutual flagellation,' which enabled her to joke: 'With all their money they could pay someone to do it for them.' I hadn't heard that one before, and we started giggling, and Jean-Marc shushed us up. Out there, the toughies bent the girl over and spread her legs for further anointing. She 'fought' violently, her pure white body writhing and her face showing terror, then she sank to the ground, to be lifted firmly onto the altar by three celebrants who held her arms and legs while she thrashed about some more. Then came incantations to Beelzebub and others, after which the chief priest produced a long ornate dagger, holding it over her heart. He stroked the now-still body all over and kissed her navel and quim. Finally he thrust the dagger into her body, and tomato juice oozed down her ribcage and onto the altar cloth.

The audience gasped and everything went black again. The gear was hastily removed and the lighting restored fully. The celebrants and muscle men walked in and took a bow, acclaimed by the public amid loud discordant organ music.

But the girl wasn't there – a nice touch.

We walked to the yacht harbour. Serge mumbled that he loved me, and I gave him a stilted smile. Was he tipsy again? He seemed as mentally screwed up as I was of late, and I told him: 'Don't drink too much or you'll be sick.' I was apprehensive and could picture us going out to sea with a drunken crew and being shipwrecked.

A portly, sallow-faced man wearing chunky rings, introduced as Clement Pharaon the boat owner, saw us up the gangplank: 'So glad you could come. Kindly remove your shoes, ladies.'

'What is this place, a mosque?' Serge wisecracked.

Pharaon glowered at us: 'Leave your shoes here, they'll be safe. Nice breeze, force 5, just what we need.'

'Sounds like *force majeure*' quoth Serge, and I jabbed him with my elbow. He clutched dramatically at the ropes.

The boat had only a few lamps burning, but the dockside lighting saw us across the deck, which was already tilting back and forth. A hi-fi system was playing 'Red Sails in the Sunset' and Aline said she felt like the young Duchess of Windsor.

A black man in a white jacket presented me with a tray: 'Champagne, madame?'

'Of course, how nice.'

Everything *was* nice. The white boat, the white awning, the white stars in the firmament. All nice, but swaying ominously. Two men, also in white, leant against the rails chatting with the skipper who wore a naval cap and now was pointing to ropes and furled sails.

I found Aline again: 'So we really are going out, and in the middle of the night! I've never set foot on one of these things in my life. When do we weigh anchor?'

'Actually we cast off, *ma chère*, although that's about the extent of my seamanship. We're in safe hands, don't worry, you'll like it.'

'I hope so. Tell me, is Pharaon a Lebanese?'

'The Pharaons practically run Lebanon, or used to. Come and meet his boyfriends.'

There were Euro-gays dressed much as we were, but with no makeup, thank goodness. They described themselves as 'reserve crew'. I also met a local councillor and his wife, an Italian hairdresser from Bordighera, a couple of Austrian popsies called Irene and Hansi, a wine merchant by the name of Andreas and a French girl called Amandine. A final group of guests came aboard and the crew began stowing the awning, hoisting in the gangplank, heaving at lines and growling at one another. The engine throbbed more loudly and, without warning, we swooped away from the quayside, only to stop about 50 metres out where the boat leapt about and sails billowed out above us.

'Should be a pleasant crossing,' the councillor remarked.

'Crossing!' I squawked.

'Yes, he wants to put into Bastia tomorrow.'

'Corsica! But that's miles away!'

'I shouldn't worry, we may never get there,' He took compassion on me. 'It'll be smoother when we are under way. We're too far inshore.'

True, after a few minutes we were gliding along without the engine and everyone was dancing in their bare feet, when they weren't guzzling at the hot buffet or swigging back cocktails.

A late guest aboard was none other than the pop singer Julien Meharet. I met up with him when we found ourselves jiving together in a corner.

'You're Julien Meharet aren't you?' I shouted. 'Nice to meet you, saw you on the box, I like your style.'

'Thanks, it's a living. To be honest I prefer Mozart, I trained with the Opéra de Paris.'

'Too much of a comic turn for me, I like Haydn.'

'That stuck-up bootlicker! What's your name?'

'Laure-Anne.'

'I read a book by Laure-Anne Something. Would that be you?'

I nodded fiercely: 'It was ghosted for me, in English. You read English then?'

'Every other word. I'm honoured, an authoress! You still in the call girl racket.'

'That's not nice. I never was. You should read more carefully.'

We stopped lurching about, and I had to answer his questions about that, then he said: 'We must get together some time, you could get some more material.'

'Why not?' He flashed his dark brown eyes at me and the demon sizzled within me.

'Let's go and look at some films,' he said.

I frowned, not understanding, but his proposal became clear when he led me into a lounge area where most people seemed to have gathered now. A small screen was showing a film of some army men who had broken into a convent dormitory. By the glow of the bulkhead light I saw the Blins and was relieved to know they were still about. Serge was dozing on his own some distance away. A couple of Pharaon's boyfriends were arguing and pinching each other. Andreas the wine merchant sat with his trouser zip undone, gently stroking himself as he stared at the screen. Irene had her skirt round her waist and was lying with legs spread on a male who looked most uncomfortable with his head askew.

A cigarette was going the rounds, and I supposed it was some drug. It reached me and I refused it, but Meharet took a pull. The floor was littered with drinks, and a glass went flying when a leg struck it. The film ended and another tape was inserted. Then Pharaon appeared with a camera and half the guests promptly hid their faces; he panned in on Irene and her victim who were in the final hard-breathing sequence.

The pop singer and I were sitting as good as gold, except that he was breathing in my ear and I could hardly bear being next to him. Every woman knows that feeling, when she wants a strange man but can do nothing about it. I could not make out whether he was breathing in my ear deliberately or just by chance. I remember he smelt of hay. Then his arm was round my shoulders and he was pulling my head towards him. Hazy from drink I let him kiss me. Wrong, so wrong! Why do we do these things!

This was my first physical contact with another man since I got married, and I was quickly trembling. Hot now for love and with Serge *hors de combat*, I let Julien fumble at my bodice as he gave me more honey kisses; his tongue slithering inside my mouth like a little mouse. I pulled back, then licked around his lips to give him the come-on. There was no stopping us now. His fingers were everywhere and I was caressing his silky chest.

Oh the temptation! My belly was aglow, I couldn't keep still and wantonly guided his hand between my legs, then into my panties. I moaned: 'Julien, Julien, it's lovely, play with your pussy cat, take me now, in front of everyone, hurry I can't wait!' I fought to undo his belt, impervious to the reprimands of conscience.

Malheur! At that precise moment a piercing scream rent the air, ending our steamy idyll. Hansi was crouching on a bunk, her eyes riveted on a spot near some glasses on the floor. We all followed her line of sight, to perceive a *snake*! Pandemonium broke out as people yelled and leapt about, but nobody approached the snake. I hastily re-clipped my bra but forsook my knickers. Jean-Marc Blin seized a cushion and prepared to do battle with the horror, while the rest of us huddled next to the door which someone was trying to open. A mighty voice bellowed from outside: 'Go back, it opens your way, go back!'

Pharaon's bulk jammed the doorway and everyone was yelling 'Let us out . . . there's a snake in here . . . stop hitting me . . . put your foot on it!' Pharaon stood his ground with upraised arms: 'Don't touch it, it's worth a fortune', and the councillor barked: 'Get it under control, *nom de Dieu*!' The Lebanese plunged in, meaning to do just that, and the crowd rushed to get out.

'Serge, Serge, where are you!' I cried above the tumult, then charged back inside to find him propped up unconscious about a metre from the snake. It was crawling slowly towards him, and Pharaon lunged about trying to keep his balance.

'Wake him up,' he rasped. 'They attack anything asleep, have to know snakes. Someone must have let him out.' He caught the pet by the head and cooed: 'There we are, Abdelaziz, nothing to worry about now, it's all over.'

I shook Serge and slapped his face. The idiot was pissed, so I eased him down flat on the bunk. A groan rumbled deep inside him, and I left with the boat owner. 'He'll sleep it off,' he said.

Outside the multitude was milling about, the lounge party explaining it all to those who had been on deck, and Pharaon staving off questions and protests.

In the disorder I found myself being edged towards the bow, isolated from the main group. And at this juncture the sea voyage took an alarming turn, for three men were cutting me off: the councillor, the Italian hairdresser and a man with a moustache whom I had not noticed so far. He was French and now demanded: 'Are you coming with us?' The councillor said: 'We won't hurt you.'

They were going to gang-bang me!!! Already the councillor had a fist round my wrist and the Italian had hold of the other arm. In the suppliant voice of his countrymen, the hairdresser said: 'You no spik, you kip still.'

'When my husband hears about this . . .'

Moustache had my bra off in seconds while the others held me. Julien had undone my buttons and my white quivering breasts now hung free, the nipples jutting out appealingly in the chilly breeze. The man slicked his belt off, and I was dragged to a tarpaulin on the deck and laid on my back. Damn Serge! After months as a loyal wife I had been forsaken by the man whose prime job was to protect me. No woman likes that kind of negligence, it makes for defiance, and I was almost glad at my predicament. I was already highly aroused, and more than ready for these three males now lusting after me. I could take them all on, if only they would stop hurting me. It would serve Serge right!

'Stop it,' I ordered. 'All right, I'll cooperate, I don't want to be maimed for life. Take it easy.'

Moustache hurriedly lowered his trousers to disclose a dark swinging shaft against a pair of white thighs. Instantly his *grosse bitte* was against my opening and he was vibrating it fast with his hand. The boat was yawing and the sea slapped against the hull. His cock was quickly rigid and he pushed hard, penetrating me smoothly as I was already loose and moist. He jogged away like a dog until his fists clasped my shoulders and he came inside me. I let out a moan of relief that he hadn't hurt me.

However the Italian mistook the reason for my huge sigh: 'You see, you like.' He took over, but had trouble achieving an erection, and to crown it all ejaculated too early the moment he reached my entrance. He spat out a curse and turned away. So much for Latin lovers!

The councillor stood confidently leering at me, unzipping himself. 'She's coming,' he said, laying a hand on my belly, a gesture that brought me to the brink of orgasm. He held back, then got the others to turn me over, and I was crouching perilously on my knees on the slippery tarpaulin, my behind in the air, my bosom a heavy udder swinging beneath me. Water by the hundredweight buffeted the boat, the wind howled, and our vessel corkscrewed its way ponderously from wave to mighty wave.

Unsteady on his feet, the councillor entered me clumsily at first, then wrapped his arms round my waist to anchor his prick. Repeatedly he lunged, his pelvis slapping against my bottom, his hands clawing at my layer of waist flesh as he finally attained his apotheosis, shooting his juices deep into my hot and hungry passage.

Considering the weather, my own climax ought rightly to have been titanic, but it was more of a nuclear meltdown. The men left me ungallantly to my own devices. I lost my grip, my knees gave way and my jellies splashed painfully onto the flat surface, as I slithered to a crumpled heap on the deck.

By which time the three rotten pigs had trotted off.

Chapter Nine

We were well and truly into one of those sudden storms for which the Mediterranean is renowned, and the rest of the excursion was a nightmare.

Bruised all over from my ordeal, I made my way amidships to find Serge glowering at me flabby-mouthed and swaying like a skittle. Again and again the bow of the yacht rose to an appalling height. Pharaon and the skipper were yelling at each other behind the wheel, two crewmen battled their way past me to the forward mast, and the sails flapped wildly as they took in canvas.

'It's a ketch, we're safe enough!' someone shouted. In fact everyone seemed to be shouting: 'We're turning back . . . must be at least force 10 . . . Oh, why won't it stop moving? . . . Amandine's throwing up, hold on to her . . . Open the door . . . Close the door!' At length we huddled in our lifejackets in the lower enclosure, awaiting instructions. The pounding noise was dreadful, the stench quite nauseating. At one stage Pharaon opened the door and barked: 'Everyone happy? It's only a squall, it'll be windy from now on, I'm turning back.'

Several people sighed with relief, then the vessel plunged like a tone of concrete and the sighs became groans. I looked at my watch, it was past 3 a.m. When we reached

Antibes I was one of the few people capable of standing upright. Beginner's luck.

The Brossards survived like everyone else, but we were prostrate all the next day. That evening, toying with a light meal of fish fillets and fennel, Serge broke a long silence.

'I've no doubt you are proud of your performance.'

Ignoring his empty glass I poured myself more wine: 'I like your cheek! You didn't care overmuch, you could have looked out for me, protected your own wife from those animals – if you'd laid off the drink as I told you.'

'I was drugged.'

'Don't expect me to believe that. You couldn't hold your drink, that was all.'

He stamped on my toe under the table, and I squeaked. He mumbled: 'This is no ordinary hangover I have. I tell you I was drugged, I could do nothing. But you chose to behave like a trollop. The whole boat was watching, you were screaming with pleasure, letting the men do it to you.'

I scowled: 'You don't imagine I invited them at ten francs a go. It happened so quickly, it was a planned thing, there was nowhere to escape to. And you made no effort. Drugged, *mon oeil*!'

He retorted: 'It was too late when I came to my senses. Anyhow I had to be careful because Aline and Jean-Marc are good friends, and Pharaon is not a character you upset. It would have been unwise to make a big scene out of it.'

'Hah, at last we've got the truth!' I scoffed. 'A rich sheikh is more worthy of respect than your poor wife. You're a weak snob, Brossard, one of the dull generality of men drawn to the moneyed classes. If you were drugged, it was because you smoked that weed.'

'When it comes to snobs, you yourself make a pretty stuck-up little bitch when you try.'

'And you're a fat pig,' I spat at him.

Serge lowered his fork and stuck his knife under my chin: 'That does it, we're leaving.'

'Without me.'

'You want to bet?'

We packed in silence, and I managed to sneak off and make a quick call to thank the Blins, saying that Serge had been summoned home to an urgent case.

At around midnight he stopped the car in a lay-by a few kilometres north of Antibes.

'Get out!' he ordered.

'But it's raining, there's mud everywhere, it's completely deserted and creepy with all these trees dripping and everything.'

His left palm thwacked my right cheek, but the blow was badly aimed and it squashed my nose. 'Get out!'

'No!'

He jumped out his side, came round and dragged me out: 'When will you learn to do as you're told? Now say you're sorry, you little cock-sucker, say you're sorry and won't ever go with another man.' I stood my ground staring at him, and he went on to mimic me: ' "Oh Serge," she says, "I'll never let another man touch me as long as I live, I'm yours for ever." ' He shook me by the shoulders and my teeth rattled. 'Married less than a year and having it off three at a time. Whore!'

'I was raped! You're completely mad!'

A second later I was sprawled face down over the car bonnet with his fingers fast around my neck. This, I realised, could be my last ten seconds before he snuffed out my crazy life. I was too close to death to shriek out, but I still remember the pain at the base of my skull and the way the bonnet ground into my hipbone. Then Serge threw me aside angrily and got behind the wheel.

I made to get in but found he had locked my door. I tapped on the window, and then to my horror he drove off without me! Genuinely astonished, I stood watching the tail lights with a sagging jaw. The Renault shimmied onto the asphalt and I expected Serge to stop and wait for me, or at least throw my coat out. Instead he accelerated and disappeared round the bend. At last I realised what was happening and yelled his name out twice, and then once more. Finally I just stood and listened.

There was silence. A van went by in the other direction, its driver doing a double-take at me but pressing on nevertheless. I sloshed about in the mud, spitting out a stream of swearwords and with good reason: my dress was soaked, my hair was in rats' tails and my shins were caked in mud.

I reached the road and began shaking with the cold. Through the steady spatter of the rain I strained my ears hoping that Serge had relented and was perhaps even reversing to fetch me. But it was now evident that the vindictive sod had simply gone off and left me, an action that was absolutely inhuman but one that was starting to make sense in view of the conversations we had been having lately.

Having avoided murder by strangulation, I was now scared of the night air; people do die of pneumonia. Miserably I scanned the darkness in the vain hope of finding some sort of shelter. Then a car was approaching on my side of the road and I turned round and started jumping and waving my arms. Anyone who had ever come across a witch-like figure thumbing a lift in mid-air in the middle of the night will readily understand why the driver failed to grasp my intentions at first sight. He probably thought I was some kind of hippie, for the car flashed by well clear of me. Mercifully the guy had second thoughts because his tyres squealed, and he came to a halt 50 metres past me. And then there was a door hanging open and the warm leather upholstery inviting me in.

'I'm so grateful,' I said hoarsely at the dapper man in the blue striped suit who was shifting his briefcase to the back seat. This time it was an even bet that my revolting appearance would save me from physical dishonour, although French men do feel compelled to exploit any superiority they enjoy over a woman. I added nervously: 'If I look enticing, go ahead at your own risk.'

'You look wet,' he said politely, which was hardly the most adventurous of opening gambits.

'That's because it's raining.'

'So I noticed, it's been raining for 18 hours.'

'That's hardly my fault.'

He moved off: 'You presumably haven't been walking about for 18 hours.'

'Hey, what's with you? Who ever walked for 18 hours?'

'This is to say I'm intrigued to know why you have been strolling around at all without a coat.'

'I gave it to a beggar 16 hours ago.'

'What's your name?'

Evading the question I said: 'I'm dirtying the floor with all this mud. Is this a Rolls Royce?'

'It doesn't matter about the floor, here take that coat of mine from the back, put it round your shoulders. No, this is a Jaguar.'

'As long as it's got a roof, who cares!'

My rescuer gave a quiet chuckle. I shifted in the seat, I was soaked through. 'Could we have some more heater? I'm frozen.'

He fiddled with the fascia panel, and nothing was said for a while. Suddenly he braked and I saw our Renault ahead of us, it was stationary. My driver swerved, and I just glimpsed Serge as we whizzed by.

'Imbecile,' the chap said in a clipped voice. 'He could have parked in the middle of the road while he was about it. They simply don't think, these people.'

'But if the car was in the middle we would have hit it,' I said, adding sheepishly: 'Oh, I see what you mean.'

The man resumed interrogating me: 'No handbag, I see. You haven't been attacked, have you?'

'Not lately. My-er-cousin and I stopped to have an argument and he drove off. He was raving mad. And now it's me whose raving mad. That was him in the Renault.'

He squinted at his rearview mirror: 'He must have seen you, and he's madder still, coming up fast behind us. Shall I hand you back to him? *Diable*, he's trying to overtake, and on a bend!'

'Don't let him, accelerate please! That's my brother, I mean my cousin. He'll kill me if he catches us!'

A pair of gimlet eyes bored into mine: 'Kill you?'

'He's-um-in the mafia,' I spluttered.

'He looks the type. What armament does he carry?' And

to my amazement the fellow flipped open a compartment in front of him and left it open. There was a gun in it!

'Steady on,' I said, 'this isn't Starsky and Hutch. I'm sure he's not armed. But he's got a grip like a vice. Goodness knows what he'll do with me if he catches me. How fast can this thing go?'

'Three hundred when I force it a bit.'

'Miles or kilometres?'

'I never found out, I don't worry about the figures, I read it in the brochure.' The Jag surged forward. 'Hundred and eighty, we'll be on the autoroute in one minute, then we'll lose him, provided the cops don't get us.'

He laughed and I laughed too: 'You don't know how funny that is.'

'Nor do you. You have a nice laugh.'

'Thank you. Everybody says so.'

We stopped at the toll as if a giant rubber band had caught us. The driver took a card from the slot and we zoomed off again.

After a minute I looked back and there was no sign of the Renault. I said: 'You know I'm really sorry, I'm ruining everything, the floor, the seat, your coat.'

'Don't worry,' he replied. 'The firm will pay. You have nice legs, too.' My dress was skimming my panties, and I flipped over a coat flap to hide myself. 'What's your name, mine's Antoine.'

'Alice,' I said, giving him the first name I could think of.

'What's your cousin's line of business?'

'Er-pinball machines, I think. He doesn't say much.'

'Interesting, you have nice eyes. Where are we heading?'

There was a big fuss about this, with him saying he was going to Paris, and me saying he could drop me at the Auxerre exit, and him saying he wouldn't dream of it and would take me home, and me saying it was kind of him and I would be very grateful if he could spare the time but he'd better not hang around because of my cousin.

We settled down for the rest of the drive. He wasn't a

bad looker, though shortish, I guessed he was about 50, with disciplined features and grey hair.

'What do you do for a living?' I enquired.

'I work for the government.' Nothing more was forthcoming and I did not probe further.

He let me out at our block of flats, I thanked him profusely, and said I must dash off and wake the caretaker to get a key. I asked him his full name in case we met up again.

'Antoine Derivry,' he said, handing me a card.

The Jag sped off and I looked at the card. Under his name were the words: '*Capitaine, Gendarmerie Nationale*'.

Chapter Ten

Serge found me in bed, rolled up in blankets and wearing a woolly hat. A couple of aspirin and a rum-and-lemon were circulating through my system and I was wet with sweat. Whatever else lay in store, I did not intend to die of exposure.

'Where did you get to?'

'What kept you? I made my own arrangements, as you noticed. Now leave me alone, I'm in no condition . . .'

'Now you listen to me . . .'

He put a knee on the bed and the mattress bounced. I growled from within the bedclothes: 'Don't try anything, I've got a long sharp knife in here, just let me sleep this off.' He said he would camp in the lounge.

The next day I woke after 9 a.m. and the apartment was empty. Half an hour later, after two bowls of coffee, I was listening to Rika Zarai on the radio. I was also breathing heavily due to a combinasion of self-pity and anger, for this was what she sang:

Je rêve d'être une femme soumise par la force et la douleur. Une servante qu'on martyrise à coups d'amour, à coups de coeur. Dans la dentelle et la soie, allongée sur les canapés, dans les bras de Casanova, j'ai envie de plonger dans l'amnésie, d'oublier à jamais que je suis une femme liberée.

(I dream of being a woman subdued by pain and suffering. A servant marytred by heartache and the pangs of love. In lace and silk, reclining on sofas in the arms of Casanova, I long to plunge into oblivion, to forget for ever that I am a liberated woman.)

This from a woman who had served in the Israeli army!

Outside the sun was shining. I opened the kitchen window and drank in the crisp March air, deciding that I had had enough of oblivion and martyrdom. Somewhere along the line Serge and I had reached a complete misunderstanding and it was useless to expect him to discuss it sensibly or do anything about it. He had to be taught a lesson.

Let me quote another of my sisters, Baronne Nadine de Rothschild:

A woman should listen to her husband, be devoted to him, be beautiful in his eyes, soft of speech, useful in his career, obedient in all her duties and above all discreet. Lightness of touch is an essential quality in a woman, and she should never weigh on a man . . . Men are created to have money, women are not, women are made to ask for it.

Within the hour I had showered, made-up and dressed, crammed some basics and biscuits into a hold-all, left my wedding ring on the table and was off to the savings bank.

I felt as much a prisoner as Ingrid Bergman in Rossellini's film *Stromboli*, when her husband nails up the doors and windows with her inside – she later escaped via the volcano. In Avallon there was no volcano but we had something better, a Route Nationale.

I walked slowly along the road for three kilometres until I came across a lorry parked on the side. The trailer was covered by a dirty grey tarpaulin but the red and blue cab was spick and span. The vehicle had a '59' registration plate which meant it came from the Lille area (it was one of the few numbers I knew). Reaching up I thumped on the nearside cab door. Behind the window a flowered curtain was drawn back to reveal a large but not unfriendly countenance of some 40 summers enclosed in bushy black whiskers. A pudgy fist slid the window open.

'Mademoiselle?' the man growled deeply, his face puffy with sleep.

'Oh dear, I've woken you up.'

He glanced at his watch: 'No matter, it's time anyway. What's your trouble?'

'No trouble, I'd like a lift. Are you moving off soon?'

'Where to?'

'Wherever you're going.'

'*Désolé, ma petite*, find yourself another client. *Salut.*'

'No, wait,' I cried. 'Take me part of the way, I won't talk.'

'That'd be a change. All right, I'll take you as far as Lyon if you like. Stay there a bit while I tidy the place up.' He disappeared, and I stood examining the front wheel which was about as tall as I was. He poked his head out: 'I'm on the Teheran run.'

'Teheran! That would be nice. Where is it?'

'Take my tip and try Lyon. It's safer, no matter what they say.'

He got out, drew some water into a bowl from a tank under the trailer and noisily sluiced his face, then wiped it with a massive orange towel. He then urinated under the semi and told me to climb up. I lifted a leg.

'Not quite dressed for this kind of thing, are you?' he said.

'Not really, but I don't have any trousers. You could always turn away if it embarrasses you.'

'A free look never did any harm.'

'That's not what they told me at convent school.' He placed his hands on my rump and gave me a purposeful shove, then handed up my bag.

He waddled round and heaved himself up behind the steering wheel, then began switching things on and pushing buttons on an array of controls that made as much sense to me as a concert organ. I kept my word and said nothing. The engine gave a bang and a roar and we moaned our way off the rough ground and onto the road. The cab shook but the din and vibration was less alarming when we got through the gear changes. We bumped up and down in unison on our seats, and I wondered how anyone could possibly go as far as Teheran and back in this fashion.

We must have travelled for ten minutes when he said: 'Cheer up.'

My head turned and I realised I had been staring wood-enly in front of me with my jaw set. He gave me a speculative smile.

'What's the date?' I asked.

'The second of March.' My wedding anniversary, my first!

'Not going on the autoroute, are you?'

A long pause: 'What have you got against autoroutes?'

'Nothing.'

After a minute: 'They watch the tolls, if that's worrying you. I'm sticking to the *Nationale*.'

'Ah.'

'Not carrying drugs?' I shook my head. 'Bombs? Guns?'

'I just want the ride.'

'The ride!'

'I've never been in a lorry before.'

'You've got a nice speaking voice, like the girls on TV.'

'Thank you. Where have you come from. What are you carrying?' It was hard work shouting.

'I come from Valenciennes, that's where I live. I'm taking valve castings, this is my fourth run and I've two more to go. I like the trip, so would you if you lived in Valenciennes.'

'Have you any aspirin by chance?'

He handed me his first aid box, and pointed to a bottle of Volvic water. I took a swig and so did he. We were caught in traffic and nothing was said for a long time. He took us past Lyon and at 3 p.m. we pulled up at a restaurant where our truck joined a dozen others.

'You can get another lift from here. Unless you want a bite to eat.'

'I'll say I do, but I'm paying.'

'Wouldn't hear of it. I make plenty on expenses. Always eat well in Europe, from Istanbul on it's a matter of luck. Anyway if you had money you wouldn't be doing this.'

'I've got some.'

'But not much. Nice having your company, Mam'selle. I'll foot this bill.'

'It would help. Thanks.'

I owed him an explanation, especially now that he was going to take me further, whether he realised it or not. As we sawed through our steaks and drank our jug of red, I asked him if he was married. He told me he had divorced three years earlier, there was one boy aged five who lived with his ex-wife. I spun him a yarn about being married to a civil servant and how it hadn't worked out and I was running away. I said I was a hotel receptionist and my husband had ordered me to quit the job, as he was terribly jealous.

'I understand, Mam'selle.'

'My name's Laure-Anne.'

'I'm Jacques Thuret, they call me Jacquot Le Bouc. Ever going back to him? They'll find you, you know.'

'Maybe. This'll bring it to a head, and if we can't argue it out I'll take the rest of my things and clear off. I can start a new life.'

'No babies?'

'No babies.' I got out my small mirror and winced at my whey face and my hair still straggly from yesterday's rain.

Jacquot was a jovial man, with some resemblance to Peter Ustinov. His amiable face now broke into a large grin and his teeth showed white through the whiskers. He leaned back a contented man, with his palms rubbing his paunch which was contained by a pair of shapeless blue trousers and a grubby white shirt. His ensemble was topped by a green muffler and a red pullover. 'Let him make his own pile, you get half of what there is if you do split up, if it comes to a divorce.' I stiffened at the word. 'In which case you'll join the club.'

'Club?'

'The singles. Fastest growing statistical group in the West. A pity in a way, but it's the trend.'

We had forged something of a bond, and thus I set out with Jacquot for Iran. He told me to keep my money and repay him when he worked out the bill and we separated. I agreed to that and insisted he write down his address at once. He refused but told me the firm's phone number was on the side of the cab. How I was ever going to pay him was another problem.

The ride through Italy was entrancing. There were so many ochre and rose villas, such a blend of colour between the soil and greenery, and there were breathtaking glimpses of the soft haze in the valleys that I had always thought artificial in the old paintings.

We spent the first two nights chastely at cheap taverns, one near Turin and the other somewhere west of Zagreb. I crossed the Italian and Yugoslav frontiers on foot, entering Yugoslavia with dollars instead of francs, as Jacquot said dollars laughed at bureaucracy and stopped people asking questions. That afternoon as we took a nap on a hillside he announced that from then on we would be kipping down in the cab or under the trailer. The first night we spent in the cab at the Bulgarian border in a lorry park.

The bunk was big enough to take two people lying close together, and Jacquot was a large man. The result was that I spent most of that night listening to engines starting up, vehicles rumbling about, and the chatter of drivers conversing in a variety of tongues. Istanbul was a repetition of this and by the time we had reached Turkey I was aching and tired, as well as being uneasy about the notorious Turkish prisons. We crossed the border at a place called Kapikule where hundreds of trucks wallowed in mud and filth. Jacquot ordered me not to stray from the vehicle and spent hours with the transit agent, handing out bribes and girlie books. After which we bowled along as far as Edirne where the mosques and minarets left me with no doubt that we were in another world; the domes resting on their slender pillars were magical. Every so often as the journey lengthened, we had to battle our way past a variety of obstacles – tractors, barrows, mules, bikes and children who waved to us.

We progressed steadily through valleys, and villages of multicoloured houses, as far as Londra outside Istanbul where we had to search for a place among two or three hundred other trucks. Here we found washrooms and returned to the cab to discover an armed guard who ordered Jacquot to shift his truck elsewhere. Jacquot argued back in pigeon English and the guard spat on him and Jacquot spat back. The three of us stood rigid until the guard finally turned away. Later, we ate at a self-service place and Jacquot said we would go to a night club.

'A night club!' I exclaimed, my surprise getting the better of my fatigue.

'Some of the lads stay here for days spending all their dough. Then they telex home for more funds, saying they've been robbed. Come on.'

It was nearly as black inside as out, but this only added to the adventure. Girls stood on tables gyrating their bellies while coins tinkled and clanged on cords round their hips. From time to time a driver or a tourist would slope off with a girl to adjoining premises. That night we were passably drunk and we threw off the covers and our inhibitions in the cab, we fell asleep locked in each other's arms and too flaked out to do anything more.

I woke to the pungent smells of goats, mint tea, cooking oil and tobacco, to feel Jacquot's trailbar jammed against my starboard aft and his beard scratching my shoulder blades; he was still snoring and I eased away from his stiff cock. He turned on his back and I had the pleasure of observing his risen appendage announcing the dawn through his underpants. His nose and mouth gave a splutter and he, too, woke up with an effort, realised that all was revealed and made to tuck in his erection. But I stopped him and gave him a soulful look.

'No, let me see it. It's beautiful.'

'I need a leak.'

'No, wait. Let me see it, full of blood and piss. I want to feel it, you're so thick and sinewy.'

He chuckled: 'Like I said, you have a nice speaking voice. But I still want a leak and you're a sadist.'

'How did you guess,' I gurgled, enveloping his pole with the fingers of my left hand. 'It makes a lovely minaret, maybe it will sound the muezzin if I kiss it.'

'Might do at that. Why do you imagine the Arab day starts at 5 a.m.?'

'Because this is when the women can have their men nice and big? All right, off you go and I'll fix the bunk.'

We were running late, so we were unable to see inside the Blue Mosque. We crossed the Ankara Bridge, now we were in Asia Minor travelling along the shore of the Sea of Marmora. At a point some 100 kilometres from Ankara, Jacquot told me to keep quiet for ten minutes. A moment later I could see why as we edged our way down a hellishly steep hill that went on and on past burnt out wrecks of vehicles that had taken the descent too fast. Jacquot kept pumping his brakes and I wiped beads of sweat from his brow.

When we were down he said: 'On my first trip the brakes overheated near the bottom and I had to zig-zag, free-wheeling between buses and trucks. Quite apart from the danger, you don't stand a chance if you have an accident. One of our blokes spent a year in jail for an accident that wasn't his fault. He has refused to leave Europe ever since. Another thing, you need to be careful in the villages because they drive their sheep under the wheels, declare triple the number dead and demand huge compensation.'

The next night, still in Turkey, was heavenly. The sky was immense, full of stars and a sickle moon, and the balmy air scarcely stirred the trees. We got the mattresses out of the truck and reclined as we ate an omelette of peppers, onions, tomatoes and garlic. The lorry was parked on flat ground so that the oil, fuel and water gauges would 'read true' the following morning.

'Complete silence, just listen to it,' I whispered. 'And at last it's cool. I wouldn't have missed this for the world.'

My companion merely nodded slowly several times, and then left his mattress for mine. He hooked his fleshy thumb and forefinger round my neck and fondled my hair. I told him: 'Thanks for letting me come with you. I am happy for the first time in ages, all my troubles have evaporated, left behind in silly old Europe. You're nice, Jacquot, I needed this trip.' I gave a long sigh.

'Let's consecrate the instant,' he said, adding a snort. 'You didn't expect to hear that kind of sentence from a lorry driver, did you? Well, you're not the only one with class, I've read things. Only a month back I picked up an old copy of Racine's *Phèdre* in Riyadh of all places. Read it far into the night.'

Placing a finger on his mouth, I said: 'Sh. What about that consecrating you mentioned? Do you often take girls?'

'Depends if I like the look of them, and their personality.'

'How about mine?'

'Best so far.'

'I'm so glad.'

I guided one of his hands to my thigh. The rest was up to him. He had been good to me in every way, and I was his if he had a mind to. 'You have delicate hands, I like the way they do things. Who would imagine you . . .'

It was enough, for his fingers were all over me in seconds, kneading my breasts, my thighs, my bottom. Then he seemed to withdraw; perhaps I was the first 'classy piece' he had ever had at his mercy and he was overawed.

In my best diction I enunciated: 'You're a decent man, Jacquot. Do let's make love, I'm sure it'll be marvellous.' I stood up and he followed suit, his fingers tumbling at the top button on my dress, then at the next and then the others. My belt buckle was loosened and the dress fluttered down. I bared his chest, removed his belt and released his trouser band. He made to pull his zip down, but I was there before him, gripping his rod.

'Your penis,' I whispered. 'I love that word, I've been fascinated by it since I was little.'

He struggled to unclip my bra and I waited passively. At last the garment fell away and he cupped my orbs reverently, his fingers gently pinching my nipples. I was careful not to move, but ran my arms round his neck so that his next move was to slide his hands beneath the waistband of my panties and grasp my bum cheeks, his organ grinding hard against my pubis. Soon we were naked and we stood there fondling each other, our embrace developing into a squeezing game in which we began to hurt each other, with me scratching his balls and he biting my nipples.

There was nothing complicated about Jacquot Le Bouc, he was an honest-to-goodness bloke touching up his latest bit of crumpet before have his poke. The simplicity of it was refreshing beyond belief after all those years spent dealing with men whose desires ranged from bondage and blindfolds to having their nappies changed.

Jacquot lifted me effortlessly onto one of the mattresses, opening my legs as he did so. The scent of earth and trees was intoxicating, and I said dreamily: 'There's a big bear up in the sky.'

'And an elephant towering over you. I once knew a fellow who had a small cock and got himself an elephant's trunk grafted in its place. He managed to hide it except at parties when they served peanuts!'

We heard a kind of cough. 'What's that?' I gasped.

'Another lorry. You worry too much.'

'There's a rustling, too.'

'Probably a wild boar.'

'A wild boar!'

'They don't attack.'

'How do you know?'

'Wild boars are all right, almost human, they have a nice disposition.'

He blocked out the sky, and I felt his cock stabbing at me. I took hold of it and gasped in wonder at its size.

'That's some gear lever you have there, Jacquot, don't you hurt me. Don't be rough, it's nicer when it lasts. Go slowly to start with. I want this to be marvellous for both of us.'

I placed his big tool where I wanted it, just as the oncoming truck changed gear; the engine whined when the driver throttled back. 'Please go on, *mon grand*,' I urged him. 'The ground's rocking like an earthquake, do put it up me. Oh that's good, I can feel it all! It's so big! Bless you for holding back – you're very thick. Not too fast now for little me!'

'Some cunts are hotter than others,' he replied as he thrust, 'if you'll pardon my Arabic, and yours is scorching. Oh, you smell delicious! I'm going to come, I can't stop, *mon dieu, c'est divin*!'

He gave an almighty lunge and I uttered a yelp as his shaft seemed to drive high inside me, up to my navel, and I wanted it to stay there filling my inner depths and swelling and swelling for ever.

'Faster,' I implored him. 'Yes, pull right back each time! Take me, harder and harder – I've never had it this good, it's been so long since . . .'

A small climax took me by surprise and I clutched at the sweaty belt of flesh round his waist to keep him inside me and enjoy his great ever-thickening cylinder throbbing and wanting me wanting me wanting me! Then I went wild, squirming and shouting rude words and he gnawed with his mouth at my neck and resumed his rhythmic thrusts.

Oh sweet Jesus, he was wresting a second orgasm from me, and I cried out: 'Keep on, keep on fucking me! Don't stop, please don't ever stop! Oh what a cock you have!'

I rocked and circled under his weight, sucking pleasure from his great tool, making it rub against the wall of my cunt each time he withdrew, and forcing it on my clit when he penetrated me over and over and over.

Suddenly a great roar shattered my joy and I looked up to see a truck thundering towards us, howling and deafening us, the brake valve spitting. I went into a panic: 'It'll run over us, I screamed, it's out of control, let me go!!!'

Jacquot simply began to laugh, his white teeth shining, holding me down by my wrists, and continuing to slam in his horn of plenty, showing no mercy. I fought to escape the satyr he had become and gulped for air, my ears hurting from the engine's roar. And then I was heaving in an almighty orgasm as the earth shook beneath me from the wheels of the truck.

As the headlights picked out our writhing, naked bodies, the truck's horn sounded two piercing blasts and Jacquot gave a final bestial shove, joining me in a shuddering climax. My vagina contracted as he delivered himself and the effect was sensational, for I could feel his hot spunk spurting far into my passage. We rolled over together, wringing the last drop of pleasure from our bodies, and I found myself on top of him. I rode his burly torso, clenching his sweating body between my thighs and burrowing my mouth in his bushy face, my own hair falling like a curtain around his head.

As the rumble of the truck died away, I rose and fell weakly on his cock, jerking to the spasms of my fading ecstasy. Finally I was still and I sank back on his hairy thighs. At that moment I fulfilled an ambition I had never achieved with any man – I dozed off with my lover's cock still hard inside me and his arms round me.

Then Jacquot was shaking me by the shoulders.

'How long have I been asleep?'

'About five minutes.' He jerked his head to one side. 'There's your wild boar. I reckon we could spare him a hunk of bread.'

But it was no good. As soon as we moved the animal planted its front legs defensively, and then scampered off. This made me sad, I was so happy and would have given it my last crumb.

Chapter Eleven

We reached the Iranian border. Iranians can be more than officious. They check each wheel of a truck on a weighscale and, if you are overweight, you have to get a special exemption or else leave some of the load behind. Much the same applies to length, a few centimetres extra reduces your speed limit to 30 kilometres an hour, and they check that you keep to it. Iranian vehicles get off scot-free, I learned.

We were OK on both weight and length, but we still had to dawdle at the border for a day and a night. My companion repeatedly played a cassette of pop songs by Stephanie of Monaco, saying he liked her pluck; she had initiative and personality and was 'rather like you in a way' or so he informed me. Jacquot also produced a book with yellowing pages which gave a complete list of Arabian amorous positions, including Archimedes' Screw, The Camel's Hump, The Ewe's Coitus and The Way of the Frog. As a change from these pastimes, we played a game of finding out each others' dislikes, Jacquot claiming that one learns more about individuals from their dislikes than from their likes.

Indirectly this got us on to politics, and Jacquot declared outright that he was a communist, taking pains to explain the difference between the Communist *Party* and the Marxist *analysis*. 'What else is there worth voting for in the long run?' he said with a shrug.

'OK, Tovarich,' I scoffed. 'That's why the *Parti Communiste Français* is on the way out, I suppose.'

He pulled out his pipe and said: 'History is not finished yet. There's no need to go into the details, but I would simply like to suggest that the Bolshevik revolution was the most significant single event in the history of mankind. The rest follows. Since 1917 capitalism has been in retreat – slumps, wars, famine, the steady stream of revolutions, crime, pollution . . .'

My head spun. 'Hey wait a minute, we're pulling out of the crisis slowly but surely.'

'Repeat that in five years' time if you dare, in ten or 15 years.'

'Well, if it's all that inevitable you'd better sign me up right now!'

It went on for a while, he had an explanation for everything, but it made a change from the Hersin-Coupignys of this world. I let Jacquot win in the end; to have jeopardised our friendship with an ideological tiff would have been silly. I needed friends badly right now.

To change the subject I demanded: 'How much longer are we going to stay here? It's downright exploitation.'

'That reminds me,' he said. 'A Polish driver told me this one. What's the difference between capitalism and communism? Capitalism is the exploitation of man by man, communism is exactly the opposite!'

He gave a big guffaw and then warned me: 'Listen carefully to what I say. The Iranians are touchy, and if there's a query you say you are on this trip as part of a clerical training course. When I have any contact with officials, you had best lie in the bunk and pretend to be sick.'

Shortly after Tabriz, he stopped to inspect the lorry and announced that we were listing to starboard.

'The load's shifted, but leave it to me. This'll take some time. I'm pulling over to those trees, you keep well away, stand over there about 200 yards away.'

With the tarpaulin off, it was obvious that the second of

111

the four straw-lined crates was out of line. He extracted a pulley system from under the trailer and a long hawser which he looped round a couple of trees, then he worked a long lever so that the hawser pulled the crate back into position. After that he tied the load again, banged the chocks under the crates and replaced the tarpaulin. It was a pleasure to watch him work so competently.

At Teheran, our destination, I was allowed no more than a peep outside when we parked in the customs ground. This was a dusty area with no sanitation and one miserable water tap where Jacquot lined up for an hour with a couple of jerrycans. From behind the cab curtains I saw kids going from cab to cab offering to buy drink, cigarettes, cameras and other contraband goods. At night there were gangs of dogs, and a variety of petty thieves on the look out for money, passports and documents they could sell.

On the third day I was let out and we did a tour of the customs. The sight was incredible: rotting food, twisted crane girders, new cars fast growing old, electronic equipment in a piteous state. I saw a forklife driver, unable to get his forks under a crate marked Solid State Inverters, simply shove them through the middle. Another lift truck actually dragged a crate behind it; this was marked 'Ceramic Insulators – With Care'.

Which only goes to show that you can do anything with the new technology.

It was a good thing we were empty on the way home, for we encountered the dying phases of a sandstorm a few hours before re-entering Turkey. Jacquot had to drive along in low gear and sometimes I had to walk ahead testing the firmness of the soil.

'If you disappear I'll know where you are, don't worry,' Jacquot said the first time. 'I'll keep my eye on you all the time.'

'Well don't blink too much,' I retorted, slouching off to prod at the ground with a long stick.

At one point, when I sank into the ground up to my knees, we used a set of perforated steel runners under the wheels, and I proudly helped in the placing of them every few metres. Another technique was to let the air out of the tyres to spread the weight of the vehicle. The loose sand, which I learned was called fesh-fesh, lasted for several kilometres. Eventually the steering went – the tie-rod had busted – but Jacquot said he always carried a couple of spares.

After the soft sand we tootled along on a straight and level stretch, and he said why didn't I take the wheel for a bit. He spent ten minutes making sure I knew the eight gears and the main controls on the 'piano' as he called the panel, and then handed over to me. I reached fourth and wanted to hand back the vehicle, but he made me go through to top gear.

In Italy we had a puncture near Padua. We were going back via Menton and the Autoroute A8 which eventually leads to Paris. The offending wheel was the inner one on the nearside twin of the tractor's back axle.

'The worst one of all, just our luck,' said Jacquot.

'How much do these things weigh?'

'Never thought. Sixty-seventy kilos maybe. No need for both of us to get dirty. This'll take a while.'

So I sat back and watched as his gorilla-like body sweated and strained to unbolt and remove the outer wheel, then the punctured inner wheel, then bring up a new one, then put the two wheels back. During this operation I started to have butterflies in my stomach wondering about Avallon and the future.

Dusk fell and that night we put up at a motel and made love in clean sheets.

That turned out to be the last time on my escapade.

I clambered back into the cab after walking through the Italian and French customs. Following which, we had travelled for about 300 yards when a uniformed man with a walkie-talkie stepped out from beside a black and white police car and signalled us to pull over beneath the swaying palm trees.

In front of the police car was an ordinary-looking one

and a couple of men in lumber jackets emerged from it and approached us, one on each side of the cab. They saluted politely.

'*M'sieur-dame, Police des Frontières, vos papiers s'il vous plaît.*'

The bloke on Jacquot's side glanced at his documents, gave them back and nodded.

My chap asked where I had come from. A brief exchange followed during which I could only confirm that I was the wife of Inspector Serge Brossard.

'Proceed,' Jacquot was ordered, and I was politely requested to accompany the *flics* in their car.

'Why?'

'We have an *avis de recherche*, Madame.'

'B-but how did you know we were coming this way?'

'Please madame, *we* ask the questions.'

Behind his beard Jacquot's face hung slack and our eyes met. He said: 'I'll wait for you here. You'll be finished with her soon, *Monsieur l'Agent*?'

The dick said: 'I should carry on if I were you. This will take a while.'

Chapter Twelve

Vengeance is a terrible thing, and the retribution meted out by my husband was absolutely horrific. And this time there was nothing that I could do about it, because the knowledge that he could find me and punish me wherever I fled reduced me to a state of total submission. The moment the frontier cop asked me my identity I had become mentally numb. Thereafter I was as putty in Serge's hands, helpless to thwart the incredible things he made me do.

This development followed on logically from our relationship prior to the Antibes episode that led to my flight. But now I was infinitely vulnerable, with as much freedom as a goldfish in a bowl. It is fair to say that the kernel of male desire lies in the weakness of the female; which normally translates into such femine adornment as high heels, alluring dresses, skirts, skimpy impractical underwear – all virtually 'imposed' by the male. However the sadist goes further than men of common clay, and is no more in control of his compulsive lust than of his own circulation, so that all his impulses are channelled into a kind of cannibalism in which joyless pleasure is tinged with cowardice. The more abject the victim, the greater the urge to inflict suffering, of course. Reason and justice are banished from the argument as anger and passion take over in frightening ways.

Serge collected me at the frontier and we drove in silence to Avallon, arriving on a Friday evening.

Next morning we were up early, and drove the Renault to a river at Nevers, where groups of men were dotted along the bank, fishing.

He had me togged out in stockings, a waspie and a shiny pink mackintosh. I wore nothing else apart from shoes.

He had thought out everything to the last detail. He told me: 'Now you can really play the tart. Walk along the towpath, and whenever you get to a man, open your mac and show yourself. This is just a start.'

'You must be mad, I'll be locked up.'

'I doubt it, no one will complain.'

'But Serge, please, it's so degrading.'

'Exactly, and you know you'll love it. Open the mac for five seconds, I'll be watching you.'

He gave me a push and I left the car. The first fisherman turned and looked at me casually. I looked back at Serge who signalled for me to get on with it. I opened the mackintosh and the man dropped his fishing rod, muttering '*merde, j'ai tout vu*'.

Another fruitless glance back at Serge and I advanced on a group of three men who were joking about the first man losing his tackle on the river's edge. They looked puzzled and I flashed again, biting my lips and looking down as I passed. One of the men walked up cockily and asked my tariff, a bold move that produced a gabble of delight from his friends.

News spread quickly along the river bank, and in no time I was confronted with an assembly of half a dozen laughing voyeurs urging me to let them have a longer look. Someone asked if I was making a film, another stepped forward and made as if to grab my tits, a third tapped his temple, shaking his head in disbelief.

I ran back to Serge and found his sport was far from over: 'You see that bench? Go and sit there, open your mac and play with yourself. They'll love that.' This I did, the

116

whole line coming up to watch me caress myself, though I made no effort to put on a performance.

At a village hardware shop on the way home, Serge bought some cord, and indoors he tied one end to our balcony rail and the other to my left ankle. Whenever he was home, I would move about the flat tied to the balcony, he said.

That same Saturday evening I confessed tearfully that I had been an idiot, had acted on impulse when I ran away, and that I was sorry from the bottom of my heart. Couldn't we kiss and make up? I said, adding for good measure that the fishing bank had been 'a just punishment'. Much good did it do me. In bed that night I cringed and tried to nestle into him as of yore, but he pushed me away. I wanted to die – whatever the future held it was going to be awful. I twisted about all night and he told me I could sleep in the living room if I couldn't keep still. The next night he told me to do so anyhow, and I lay on the sofa working out a hundred ways of escaping.

'Stop that grizzling,' he snapped.

I went up to him and stood forlornly by the bed, draped in a blanket: 'I've said I'm sorry, please forgive me, I want your arms about me and your kisses and everything. I'll make it good, it'll be better than ever before. It always is after a quarrel.' There was no answer. I yelled out: 'Serge, I want to fuck you!'

'Who said the quarrel was over? I would never dream of touching you again, Lord knows where you've been. Go and find yourself a cucumber in the fridge!'

'Well really!' I exclaimed.

Silence descended upon us, and we came close to communicating just through scribbled notes. So that was that – no love, no kisses, no affection, not even a gram of respect for a fellow human being.

By the Monday morning when Serge left for work, I wanted to creep under the carpet and moulder away, but I embarked on a flurry of housework, hoping against hope that things would get back to normal that evening. Who knows, I thought, Serge might even return and fling off his clothes in the hall, hungry for love once more?

He arrived at 7 p.m. in the company of Sylvain Hersin-Coupigny, and what ensued is hard for a balanced person to understand. It is not easy to convey the mixture of guilt and cowardice I felt, for one has to have gone through it oneself. Why does one really say, in effect: 'Yes, I did wrong – punish me'? Can one *explain* the abject condition that can make a woman weak at the knees, mentally screaming out to be hurt?

When they came in it was obvious that they had devised something special for me. Serge hung back in an odd manner and SHC did not offer to shake hands; true he was hampered by what I immediately realised was a tape recorder.

'Turn round, *pisseuse*,' Serge ordered, and I had to stand with my back to them in my workaday brown skirt and cheap sleeveless taffeta top. They took my arms casually and guided them behind my back. Before I knew it I was in handcuffs. Serge told his visitor: 'I'll leave you with her, *mon ami*.'

Sylvain gave me a little push and we were in the bedroom with the door shut. He set the tape recorder going in one corner, placing my back to the only unfurnished section of the wall.

For a full minute he gloated over me. This time he wore a dark grey suit. His close-cropped hair had been cleverly dyed but the stratagem did nothing to compensate for his loose old-man's mouth and the sneer lines either side of it. Yes, he was a business magnate all right, but his weak character clearly shone through.

A glance at the tape: 'Well now, young lady, I understand you are a typist at our Clamecy works, and I see that you are in the invoicing department.' So the scene was to be harassment in the workplace, a re-enactment as it were of the incident with the secretary in the town hall, but this time he would achieve his ends!

'What is all this I hear about your misbehaving during the lunch break? You were found in a compromising position with one of the apprentices, I have been informed. We can't have that sort of thing, you know, and I understand you have been indulging in these practices for some time.'

He advanced a hand and fingered my skirt. 'What have you got to say for yourself, hm?'

'I'm afraid I have nothing to say.'

'*Monsieur Le President*,' he prompted.

'*Monsieur Le President*.'

I had been tricked, I now knew. When they put the cuffs on I had assumed it was for a whipping or some other punishment. Now it dawned on me that he was probably going to poke me. Serge was lending out his wife!

The big boss moved away and paced the small area by the bed, as he had certainly done hundreds of times in his office when reprimanding staff. 'You realise that you will never find other employment in this area.'

'*Oui, M'sieur*.'

'And you need your job.'

'*Oui, M'sieur*.'

He moved in on me again, running a finger over my shoulder: 'There is no excuse, you know. It would be such a pity to lose you, as they tell me your work has given satisfaction. And you're an attractive young woman. I could overlook the incident this time if you promise it will never occur again. But – and as I said you are very pretty – you must make it up to me, you understand. A kiss, for example, from those pouting lips of yours.'

He acted at once on the idea, his mouth chasing mine, seeking my lips awkwardly as I moved my head this way and that in an attempt to avoid him. His jacket was off in a jiffy and he clasped my waist. The bluge in his trousers was pressing into my mound, my front arching out because of my manacled fists between me and the wall. I was in his power, but I, too, had power over him, for he wanted me urgently, yearned to do what he had always wanted with a member of his female staff.

I gave a little whimper and he continued, as much for the tape recorder as for me: 'You must be nice to me.

I want to feel your firm young breasts. How beautifully sculptured they are. How inviting they look as they strain against that shiny material.'

He pawed impatiently at my bosom and I pleaded: 'Oh no, you mustn't, please don't, *M'sieur*.'

'You'll have to submit or it's the factory gate for you. I've noticed you crossing the yard, your tits bouncing, and I've always wondered how I could get into your knickers. Come now, a little feel under your skirt won't kill you.'

And the scrabbling began there and then as with trembling fingers, he stroked between my breasts, joggled my tits and fiddled at my blouse buttons, finally tearing the material in his haste. My bra came off, and he pawed my breasts, then returned to my thighs, forcing a leg between the knees and waggling his fingers at my crotch.

The running commentary resumed: 'Let's have your panties down now, slowly so slowly. I know how you women adore the feel of them coming down over their hips and legs.'

I sought to escape his attentions but he insinuated a finger into my pussy and held my neck in a powerful grip.

'Please stop *M'sieur*, I feel so ashamed . . .' His arm pumped away under the billowing skirt.

'You're coming on,' he panted, 'you are starting to like it, you see.'

He undid his trouser front and shoved his stiff cock at my thatch, rubbing it along my slit. My ankles were imprisoned by my panties and I began falling sideways.

'Take your foot out,' he muttered, and there was no choice. My legs parted as I kept my balance, and he pushed his penis in, heaving up and down, bumping into me while my handcuffed fists banged again and again on the thin wall.

Finally Hersin-Coupigny dragged my limp body onto the bed and thrust into me like a mad beast, sucking wetly on a nipple. As he grunted out his climax he kept mumbling, 'little typist, young woman, young woman . . .'

Afterwards he lay heavily on me, then got up to switch off the tape machine. He made me keep still while he dressed, then he joined Serge in the living room. My husband ordered me to stay in the room until SHC left, bearing off the record of his infamous conduct to some secret *cache*.

In a separate development I was forbidden to open the mail.

This ruling stemmed from a letter the pop singer Julien Meharet had sent me, presumably having obtained my address through Pharaon and the Blins. The missive, which was of course highly dangerous, read:

> My dear Laure-Anne,
> I simply must write to you. I lost track of you on the boat but hope you ended that eventful night without mishap. My heart leapt the moment I set eyes on you, and I cannot get you out of my mind. You are the most adorable creature I have ever had the good fortune to meet, and I must see you again, have your laughing eyes gazing tenderly upon me, touch those lips that take my breath away, hear your captivating voice. I am in love with you. Please phone me, as I don't dare call you. Ring my agent on XXXXXXX – as soon as you can. Please.
> Your devoted J. M.

A minstrel who apparently wrote his own lyrics! I stuffed the letter in a half-empty packet of lentils, but later read it about 20 times, thinking of Julien's curly locks and wondering how we could fix up a tryst.

My spouse subsequently discovered it in the food cupboard and set a match to it. The mail-opening ban followed.

In retaliation I hunted high and low for Serge's account books, to no avail. Since the SHC session I suspected he might try pimping, actually obtaining monetary reward from exploiting my body, the more so since he had stopped exploiting it himself. No doubt he kept the accounts at the Commissariat or in a safe deposit. Eventually I realised I was being silly, as he would certainly be paid in banknotes.

Further evidence that he was procuring came during a visit to the doctor, the same one as had diagnosed that I was anaemic.

'I don't need a doctor,' I objected. 'Except that you don't love me any more. You don't even kiss me now.'

'The appointment's at 7.30 on Tuesday. In the morning.'

'That's an odd time.'

He flew into a rage: *'Bon dieux de bon sang!* Why do you have to argue all the time? Just do as you are told!'

There was not a soul about when Serge put me down at the surgery door in the tight black suit, pillbox hat and red underwear I had worn frequently at the apartment. On instructions I had applied lots of perfume.

Dr Bessagnet was a short, slightly built man of about 60 with a weasel face and a tendency to emphasise every two or three words. He walked with a limp and wore thick glasses.

'Come in, come in, Madame Brossard,' he bleated. In his consulting room, one of several at a clinic run by a group of doctors, he offered me a low armchair where I sat unavoidably displaying my legs. At that stage I possessed no firm evidence that the appointment was phoney, and even my fancy togs may have been merely one of Serge's spiteful pranks.

'How's the amnesia?' the doc said as he flicked through my file.

'It seems better, Doctor.'

He coughed: 'Your husband saw me, and says you are experiencing heat flushes.'

'I hadn't noticed.'

'He says you are nervous, emotionally overwrought. Can you think of any reason for that?'

'No, Doctor.'

'Are you happy? I mean, does he-er-meet your emotional and-er-and physical needs?' My knees seemed to mesmerise him.

'Yes, Doctor.'

'You can be frank with me. Is he a loving and attentive husband?'

122

'Yes, Doctor.'

'It's quite normal for a young woman of your age to have a healthy sexual appetite. How often do you-er-make love? When did you last make love?' He gave me a rapacious stare.

'I forget, Doctor. Six weeks.'

There was no doubt now, the lecher was paying for me, I was certain. I was sullen, torn between rushing out and fixing an immediate appointment with Serge's woman boss, and playing along until I had enough evidence to lose him his job and put the bastard behind bars for ten years. Maybe I would just ruin the sod for life, mutilate him with a meat knife. Other exploited wives had done as much. I hesitated.

My crimson cheeks and wide eyes must have impressed the medic, for he went on: 'My poor lady, I quite understand, I quite understand. So frustrating, but it's nothing to be ashamed of.' I made an attempt to look shy, Bessagnet fidgeted in his chair, building up a morning erection, his eyes gleaming through the thick lenses. Here, I knew, was a predator about to realise a fantasy he had been perfecting during 40 years of probably unimpeachable medical practice.

'I'd like to examine you, take your pulse and so on. If you'd move over to this examination table, please. Take your clothes off, there's no need to use a cubicle, there's no one about.'

Slowly I removed my gloves, hat and jacket, then reached for my skirt clip.

'Let me help you,' the old chap said, eager to help.

The skirt fell around my ankles.

'Don't be ashamed. Now the blouse, and your panties. You can leave your stockings on. Sit on the table please.'

He took my blood pressure, prodded me with his stethoscope and manipulated my breasts.

'Lie on your tummy,' he said.

Apart from my stockings I was in the nude, and he ran his hands over my naked body, concentrating on the inner thighs and palpating the cheeks of my bottom.

123

'A lovely figure, nice hair.' He turned me onto my back. 'Does this hurt? And this?' He reached the copse between my thighs and prodded. I told him it didn't hurt there either.

He stood back: 'The pulse is a little high, 16–11, and your heartbeat rather fast. Now we must look at the inner works, as it were. Hrumph.'

Without a by your leave he had my legs folded back on my belly and was stroking my labia. 'How nice and soft, I'll just put a glove on.' The rubber glove snapped into place, he dipped into some cream and inserted a digit into my cunt. His lips drew back: 'You're nice and juicy, that's good.'

Now he had two fingers inside me and was running his thumb gently against my button.

'Do you do this to yourself sometimes?' he asked. 'It's normal of course.'

'Oh no, Doctor,' I said, 'at least not often.'

He found the ridge behind the clitoris. 'Oh, Doctor,' I whispered.

'All quite normal for a young woman of your natural vitality.' He panted.

I jolted when he squeezed the whole mound and clitoris: 'Doctor, I think I'm . . .' His busy fingers moved faster, wanking me without pretence.

'Ah, I see,' he muttered. 'Well, we can't leave you in this condition, it would be bad for you, you must have release.' He threw off his jacket and dropped his trousers and pants. His stiff grey probe pointed at me, then the table dropped lower as he turned a wheel.

'Doctor, I feel weak . . .'

He replied: 'This won't hurt.'

And with remarkable agility for his age he clambered onto me and within seconds was jogging away inside me. The examination table rocked perilously. He came quickly, spittle forming on his lips and falling onto my throat. Then he slid off as nimbly as he had climbed up.

His arms and fingers shook as he donned his clothes, and I suggested: 'Don't you think you ought to lie down, you're as white as a sheet.' With an artful look I added: 'You should not have done that, should you? It wasn't part of the examination, was it? You were taking advantage of me, and that was very naughty of you.'

'You may dress now,' he snapped. 'Well, Madame Brossard, there is nothing organically wrong with you. Perhaps we should fix another appointment in a week's time.' He looked as if he needed at least a week to recover.

'I'll have to ask my husband.'

'Of course, I'll be in touch with him, if you like. Take this prescription – pills for the blood pressure, you understand.'

'Thank you doctor, I understand.'

I took the sheet of paper, snatched up my bag and left without a word. My pimp was waiting in the car 50 yards down the road.

Chapter Thirteen

May came along, '*le joli mois de mai*' as they called it in the Middle Ages, but it was far from *joli* for me.

Desperately I strove to take stock, to keep sane. As may be imagined, I was listless and lacking all gumption, neurotic. One of the escape routes I had been mulling over was suicide, but I tossed it out, not so much due to strength of character as through the absurdity of the idea. I was 30 years of age and people do not end their own lives at 30; possibly at 16 or 76, but not at 30.

We had been married 14 months and, unless there occurred some miraculous change of fortune, the venture had ground to a sorry end. I was waking up to this fast. In the final analysis there is usually one partner who loves less than the other, until the other person realises it. One can be intelligent and naive simultaneously, and in our case I had, in a very real sense, become Serge's prisoner not simply his willing playmate and sex object. Where he was getting *his* sex now was a mystery; perhaps he was a natural bedjumper and had been concealing this for 14 months – anything was possible, in spite of his high moral stance on fidelity earlier on.

However, at this point my concern was not for *his* future but my own. The survival instinct was surfacing, meaning survival with sanity. Oh sure, I could buckle down and await events, but not for long. Some 90% of the human race suffers from this kind of terminal *ennuie* which, as Baudelaire has warned, 'would make a waste land of the Earth and swallow the world in a yawn'. I refused to accept that, and sensed that I would shortly have to grasp the nettle.

Meanwhile I reluctantly yielded to another command from my *maquereau* of a husband, through the continuing influence of Hersin-Coupigny, who had become a Member of Parliament in the March 1986 election.

'Laure-Anne,' Serge enquired with unusual courtesy, by way of introducing the subject, 'have you any strong religious views?'

'Obviously not, or you would have noticed. I wouldn't march in the streets about it, either way. Who knows, there might be something in it, and if there's something in it there might be a lot in it.'

He vouchsafed a humorous snort: 'Have you any objection to going with religious people, for example an abbess?'

'A what!'

'An abbess. She likes young women.'

'Is this a joke?'

'Not at all. She's a pal of Sylvain's. How about it?'

'Why should I? You've been treating me to a living hell for weeks.'

He ignored the objection: 'Hersin-Coupigny is a man whose wish is most people's command, and that must include you, *ma chère madame*. If we don't cooperate he could make big trouble for us. It's only this once. Do this for me.'

'For you! What do I get out of it?' He could not have looked more dumbfounded, and he thought for a while, before coming up with: 'She may give you a glimpse into heaven, put in a good word for you.'

'How old is she?'

'Sylvain didn't say.'

'How could he hit back at us?'

'Any way he likes. He's powerful, better to have him as an ally, we're committed already.'

'Not me, I'm not.'

'I have accepted on your behalf.'

'I bet you have.' I gave a shrug. 'All right, let her come.'

'No, *ma petite*, it's you who will be going to her, at her convent.'

'For pity's sake, how will you smuggle me in?'

'She will be interviewing you about your vocation. A heart-to-heart chat behind closed doors. An ingenious cover.'

'Ha! Just your style, you'd love to dump me in a nunnery!'

In point of fact Mère Agnès was a peach. About 65, possibly older, she was a plump, kind-faced woman with bright eyes. She held sway somewhere near Dijon, where I was shown into a sparsely furnished cell to find the abbess in a fetching coffee-coloured habit with a white cowl over her veil and a rope tied round her middle. She looked regal.

'Laure-Anne, hello!' she cooed in a turtledove voice.

'*Bonjour, ma mère*,' I said respectfully, kissing the gold ring on her finger.

'So glad you could come and see me. How about a pick-me-up? You will find some Gevrey-Chambertin and glasses at the back of that cupboard.' There were three full bottles and a half empty one which I extracted and poured from. 'Monsieur Hersin-Coupigny keeps me supplied, such a thoughtful benefactor.' And a cunning vote-catcher, too, thought I.

She raised her glass and declared: '*Tchin-tchin*'.

'*A la vôtre*.' I responded, and we took a good swallow. The old lady's round friendly face beamed and she said: 'Good year, '82. When we reach the next world I'm sure that the only sins we shall have on our conscience will be those things we ought to have done. Appreciating good wine is one of them. It's our duty to get the most out of the years we are granted. Come closer, *ma fille*, how old are you?' She strutted over to the door and turned the key in the lock.

'Thirty, *ma mère*.'

'A beautiful age, the threshold of maturity. You have

fine delicate hair, nice clothes, too.' At Serge's instruction, I had selected an imitation ripple-silk dress in Venetian red; it had a flattering bodice and finely pleated skirt. I wore a brown belt with a gold clip, circular gold earrings and a couple of gold bracelets.

'Yves Saint Laurent,' I told her.

'I read about him. Didn't he pose naked for one of his own advertisements?'

'I believe so.'

'Very odd, what merchandise was he trying to sell?' She laughed extravagantly. 'No matter, I personally prefer the company of the fair sex.'

'So I understand.' The old dear slid her china-white hands under my hair, making it flare out, then she kissed my brow and slid a hand down my back as far as the upper curves of my lumbar region.

She drew me to her: '*Mon enfant*, how fresh and fragrant you are, like a dewy yellow rose. We of the communities are starved of bodily contact. Lean your head on my shoulder.' Her eyes were a few centimetres from mine when she said this, and the message was loud and clear. I nestled into her neck and her girth made me lean into her soft and generous form. She fingered the back of my dress, playing with the material. 'So soft, *ma petite fleur*, so warm and vibrant.'

'You seem rather hot-blooded yourself, *ma mère*, and no novice in sensual matters, if you don't mind me saying so.'

As an answer she held my face in her hands and pressed her dry lips to mine. They grew moist and there was little else I could do but kiss her back. Besides, I am sentimental about older people, they seem so wise but are sad at the years that have passed them by and their failure to seize their chances. Perhaps the abbess was right about things we ought to have done.

We heard a shuffling in the corridor and I stiffened, but she told me to ignore it. We kissed a couple more times, while she softly pressed my behind, then she shifted her attentions to my groin. 'How thin this fabric is, I can feel your things underneath. May I see them, I want to see them.'

Eyes bright, she pushed me away gently and slid her fingers into my V-neck to look at my bra. 'Primrose, I knew it,' she enthused, unfastening the garment and tugging it free with an experienced pull. She cupped my breasts and sighed: 'So very round and firm, you must be proud of your bulging teats. Mine were like it once, but no boy or man ever fed on them. Nor any girl alas, and it's too late now. You know I was *directrice* at a school in Nantes for years, and I longed to touch the girls' little titties, but I did not dare and had lovely dreams instead, it was almost as good. A few of the older girls found out about my preferences and they used to try and provoke me, taking my hand, but I had to be so careful. One of them even confided in me and confessed things; she poured out such intimate details that I'm sure she did it as a bet. Would you like me to hear your confession?'

Unsure of the right response I played for time: 'I've never heard of a woman hearing confessions, is that part of the liberation theology they talk so much about?'

'It ought to be, we would do it so much better. I'm sure God is a woman; only a woman would run things – how shall I say? – in so haphazard a fashion.' She chuckled gaily. 'Now do tell me, when did you last go to confession?'

'Ages ago.'

She whispered: 'Never mind, tell me your sins.'

'W-e-ell, I wouldn't know where to begin.'

'Start with self-abuse, everyone does it. How do you bring yourself off?'

I gulped: 'With an umbrella handle, a hairdrier sometimes, or my husband's electric razor.'

'Sounds dangerous to me. What else?'

'The washing machine,' I said, thinking it up suddenly.

'Really, that's a new one on me!'

'I put it on final spin-dry and lean against it.'

'How many times?'

'Often. Three times.'

'Three times a week!' she exclaimed.

'No, a day,' I said on the brink of laughter.

She frowned in annoyance at this, and changed the subject: 'Are you a believer? You aren't taking this seriously, I'm afraid.'

I pouted. 'I'd like to be, I loved the gospels at school. But I'm a two-and-two-make-four person, and if anyone tells me they hope the answer's five, I can't go along with them.' An embarrassed smile accompanied this statement.

The abbess had inched up my dress and was stroking my stockings. 'You are very sensitive, *ma fille*.'

'I am. But isn't what we are doing dreadfully wrong – and during confession too? How can you reconcile these – er – Byzantine morals with your beliefs?'

She cleared her throat: 'There is nothing wrong with affection between women, nothing against it in the Bible or canon law, and frankly I have no intention of raising the issue with higher authority. I am a Christian woman, not given to nirvana and suchlike nonsense; I would prefer to contemplate your navel rather than my own!'

I burst out laughing, whereupon she drew me down beside her on a little couch she had in an alcove, and kissed me again, seeking out my tongue with hers. I relaxed my body and she manoeuvred us so that I was kneeling astride her legs.

'Laure-Ann,' she murmured, 'I am overcome, I must ask you something. Go to the cupboard, you'll find some honey on the left. Bring it to me.'

This I did. Then she made me stand in front of her and hold up my dress. With practised dexterity she slipped off my panties and coated my quim with honey, after which she lay back on the couch and directed me to place my knees on either side of her head, so that my fleece was suspended over her mouth. There was no need for further instructions and I sank down carefully until she could lick me.

'Are you liking it?' she enquired at length. I was too bewildered to answer, and she began nibbling me, simultaneously pushing my right hand behind me and guiding it between her own legs. 'Please, *ma chérie*, do it to me! I can never tell if it might not be the last time. Put your lips there.'

I shifted around to find that she had the rough material of her habit gathered up around her waist. I burrowed between her big, butter-soft thighs and milked her button gently with my lips. Finally she emitted an enormous groan and slipped into a trance.

It was over, and I made to leave.

'You'll come and see me again, dear Laure-Anne?'

'Of course I will. I've grown rather fond of you, Mère Agnès.'

We chatted for a few minutes as I cleared up. Then I unlocked the door, blew her a kiss and found my own way out across polished woodblock floors amid an odour of soap and lilac.

I knew I would never forget that likeable old lady so naughty and so afraid of losing her appetite.

Chapter Fourteen

Finally I acted. It was the furniture polish incident that did it.

A plastic container of furniture polish slipped from my hands onto the hall carpet. It split open down one side and the contents spilled out. I charged into the kitchen and got a big spoon and a bowl but the stuff went everywhere. I had visions of Serge charging in from the lounge, where he was sorting out papers, and yelling: 'What are you spreading furniture polish on the carpet for?' And I would snarl back: 'Me? I do this every day, at last you've noticed!' At the time the notion seemed so comical that I began shaking with amusement. So much so, that my fear now was that Serge would come in, find me spreading polish on the carpet *and* laughing my head off like an imbecile! This seemed even funnier.

In fact he heard and suspected nothing, but the interlude was sufficient, along with the charming hour I had spent with Mère Agnès, to bring me to my senses. It came as a flash to me that another, normal world existed in which people enjoyed ludicrous incidents and shared affection.

My decision was made, and I walked in and stood over Serge: 'Please remove this rope. I want to talk seriously.'

Serge held my gaze, his eyes black with venom. Moving

to the window I continued: 'Just this once, it's important. I want you to hear me out, it's important.'

'So you said.' It was 10.30 on a blustery morning in the late May of 1986. He untied the cord from my ankle and the other end from the balcony. The curtains billowed into the room and he closed the window.

'Thank you. Unplug the phone.' I got us both a drink, and pulled up a chair for myself. Cucu the cat stared at me and for once I averted my eyes irritably.

I began. 'Serge, I've had enough. I don't need to remind you that I have encountered every imaginable type of man, but I married you because I believed that at last I had met the one person I could live with for the rest of my life. I sold the club and became your wife, prepared to do anything you wanted because I loved you and was loved in return – something not to be taken lightly.

'No, don't interrupt, let me stumble through this. I want to be completely honest and say that I believed I could satisfy my sexual and emotional needs as your little woman, while bringing you equal joy. I believed that women were created to seduce and gratify men. Call it masochism and I won't argue. I sacrificed a career because I was sure we were perfectly matched. Yes, I know the word is high-flown but sacrifice is what it comes down to, because I decided not to continue in the club business and perhaps move into shows, fancy catering – who knows. I may not have been the world's top manager but I would have made it. I was learning fast, so fast I could see the money piling up. But I was scared, because I would have been a success by 40, bored by 45 and soured by the age of 50.'

I asked Serge for a cigarette and he gave me one. I poured myself another drink, his was untouched.

'Since when have you been smoking?'

'Since about 16, on average a packet a year.'

Two pulls on the cigarette and I went on: 'I fell in love with you the moment you walked into the club. I liked your style, I liked your looks, I liked your voice. At last I thought I had met someone I could admire and look up to. We made love and got married, the honeymoon was

134

unforgettable, and it was fun after that, too. I was thrilled to be setting up home with you, doing everything to please you from cooking your meals to cleaning your shoes, delighted beyond measure that I could be your servant in every way, agreeing to your every whim, willing to die for you – no, I'm not exaggerating – and above all I was so intensely proud that we were Laure-Anne and Serge, a real couple, for everyone. It was 'we-us' for a whole year, deep inside of me, longer if you count the run-up to the wedding. And now it's 'I-me' again and I hate it. I trusted you completely, thought we were going in the same direction, knew that you would look after me, come what may. Now I'm on my own again.'

His face gave nothing away, and I continued: 'Let's be clear about what has happened. It was the perfect union, we had full agreement, a firm bond, a profound understanding. Until you brought others into the act. You were forcing the pace, but I was still yours and I told myself that I had made a vow and, if you needed more excitement, then I was willing to cooperate. I was under your spell, even though you decreed that I should live without money, without freedom of decision, without transport or any independent activity.

'I've worn what you wanted me to wear, and even as recently as the session with Dr Bessagnet I walked back in that saucy outfit and it gave me a thrill because I was doing it for you. I was still fooling myself that nothing had really changed and that we could work things out.'

'What's your complaint then?'

'I've had enough, it's no good. Right now I'd be happier on Devil's Island.'

'Is that where you were aiming when you went to Iran?'

I ignored the crack: 'Up to that time you were still my high-calibre cop of a husband, the man who quickened my pulse. I hoped you would sense that we were in the danger zone, I wanted us to move onto something broader. Naively, as I now realise, I wanted to provoke you into a crisis, and I ran out, praying with all my heart that you would get me back on a new footing. OK, I lost my head. The fact is I needed air.'

'And yet another prick.'

'That's mean and silly, it's not true and you know it. The only prick I need is yours, when it pumps out true love. I had an emotional problem, and when you collected me at Menton you behaved like a petty Napoleon and decided to make me pay for my escapade. You stuck a label on me instead of realising how lucky we were, and how we could make it better. I love you Serge, and never more than at this moment when we're sitting here as a proper couple, talking about us.'

'It's you doing the talking. Carry on.'

'I asked you to listen, that's true. I do love you Serge, basically nothing has changed. Only it's not fun any more. Serge, *mon amour*, I feel so lonely, I'm scared of losing you, I . . .' The tears welled up and I broke off mumbling absurdly.

I began again with a lump in my throat. 'Serge, *mon mari*, we can start again surely! I'm your fireside lover, remember? We're like – like close enemies instead of friends. I'm sorry to grizzle like this, it's not really me, it's the tension coming out. You don't seem to realise that I can only take so much. You don't know what it's like to be dictated to on everything: what meat or fish I should buy, where we should sit on the beach, who we have in to dinner – every blessed detail. I think I'm going mad, we're strangers and I don't know what to do about it. If I don't sort myself out I'll finish up in a mental home. I feel I'm almost in one already.'

In the long silence that followed my hands pressed my temples, then he said: 'I don't believe a word of it, you're simply wrapped up in your own ego, nothing else counts for a woman anyway. I'll tell you what's happened, you've lost interest, "the past is the past cheerio I'm off". Do you imagine this is some kind of TV series? There's something behind all this . . .'

'No! Don't pull away. For God's sake, Serge, I'm throwing myself at your feet!'

136

'Like you've thrown yourself at others, on the boat, at a goddam truck driver!'

'You're twisting it all round. I've been a fool, but I was in such a state. For pity's sake, I've never been married before, I don't know how to handle . . .'

'You're a promiscuous woman, Laure-Anne.'

In a flash of anger I retorted: 'A promiscuous woman is an unfulfilled woman searching for something she can't find. Please Serge, take me back, let's stop fighting, we're grown people and we can conquer this, it's only a crisis. All I ask is normal happiness, for both of us!'

He raised his eyebrows: 'You're asking for the moon. The dream's shattered, and when that happens . . .' A shrug. 'You can't expect me to take you in my arms and forgive and forget. On your side you might forgive, but you'd never forget, you'd wait for the next argument and then take back your forgiveness. You'd be following my every move, waiting to pounce. I'm not an idiot, you know.'

I was taken aback, surprised and resentful that he refused to concede his part of the blame: 'I'm only asking for a second chance, I won't crowd you . . .' My voice trailed off, we were bumping on the rocks, already shipwrecked. There had to be a more serious reason why he was rejecting my bid for peace.

'And for goodness sake stop crying,' he barked. 'I've got problems too, that's what women never understand.'

'Then why don't you tell me about them? That's what a wife is for!'

He got up angrily. 'I don't think this is the moment. I need space too, you know. In any case, you're playing a double game, you can't be a martyred wife and have everything on your own terms. I'm sorry, you've got me as mixed up as you are. I'm going out!'

And that was that. He flung a jacket over his shoulders and stalked out.

'*Merde*!' I hissed.

Then I, too, went out, and sat in a nearby bar, realising after the second whisky that to my horror I had already accepted defeat and was wondering how I could make out on my own. The worst had come to the worst, and suddenly I didn't care. It dawned on me bitterly that not once had he so much as hinted that he still loved me.

I returned home in a haze of drink, drew the bedroom curtains and fell into an uneasy slumber.

Some kind of escape mechanism was at work, for every time I stirred it was to worry that I had not repaid Jacquot Le Bouc, and could see no way of ever doing so.

The phone bell woke me up. It was Serge.

'Sorry I left in a hurry,' he declared blandly. 'Look, I'm bringing someone back for dinner.'

My brain fought to make sense of this information which was totally at odds with the events of earlier that day. My throat and mouth were parched, my head felt as if it were stuffed with cotton wool. I squinted at the bedside clock – nearly 5 p.m. I must have slept more deeply than I thought.

'Actually, it's Liliane.'

'Who is Liliane?'

'Liliane who lost her husband, remember? If you could just do something simple. Hullo-hullo, are you still there?' There was something wrong with his tone of voice. It was friendly, as friendly as if nothing had happened!

'Yes, I'm here, I'll see what they've got at La Pêcherie Dieppoise. Perhaps I'll do a *lotte à l'américaine*, then an *île flottante*.'

'Oysters too,' he ordered. 'The milky ones, not green ones.'

'Well, all right.'

I had to put down the receiver, shaking my head in perplexity. Why should he bring anyone home after storming out like that? And why Liliane of all people?

The evening was ill-starred from the outset.

The fishmonger only had green oysters, so I got a big live crab instead, something I would never have chosen had I not felt so jaded. The man's wife told me in detail how to prepare the thing, but I never got round to it.

The wretched crab escaped while I was otherwise

engaged, and ran under a small Louis XIV reproduction chest we had in the hall. I grabbed a dustpan and tried scooping it up, then the cat darted out of the lounge to play with it before beating a retreat. I vowed to bash the damn crab to pieces with a hammer when I had it at my mercy. Time was moving fast, and then I thought of the firetongs, a superior weapon if ever there was one! But the crab was sober and I was fuddled, so I had to effect a temporary withdrawal. Trying not to be sick I resumed the contest precisely as Serge and the Lady Liliane arrived; they found me on all fours still in my bathrobe poking about under the chest with a broom handle, while the flowers on the top trembled and shed their petals.

'What's going on?' Serge whined.

'I'm catching a crab, isn't it obvious?'

'If you say so. Hey what's the cat doing sniffing about on the stove?'

'Oh lord, the *lotte*!' I exclaimed, rising scarlet-faced and charging into the kitchen.

'Well, you'd better forget the crab.'

'But we can't just leave it there!' I wailed, shooing Cucu away.

'I've got it,' Serge barked, holding the crustacean aloft. 'You merely had to shift the chest. Find me a saucepan with a heavy lid.' It was too late to cook it now. I hurriedly washed my hands.

In the lounge, Liliane stood next to Serge waiting to be greeted properly. Serge wore his best black trousers and a dark blue leather jacket. Liliane was showing off in a knee-skimming white muslin dress and navy blue underwear that could be seen through the material. I gave her a distainful smile and we shook hands with only the thinnest veneer of politeness; the widow looked down her nose at my wrap as if a large stain had appeared down the front. I swallowed, wanting to retch.

In the normal way, nothing would have surprised me at this stage in the proceedings, but Serge's next remark threw me completely.

'You must be punished for that,' he said.

'For what?'

'The crab.'

He was slow getting the words out, and it was now obvious to me that they had both been drinking, quite heavily too. Since I also felt like death warmed up I was about to suggest that, as we were all in poor shape, we might go out for a walk, when he added: 'What shall we do with her? A whipping don't you think?' Liliane declined to answer, standing completely motionless and with an uncommitted expression on her face.

Backing away, I pushed my arms forward, palms facing Serge: 'No! No you don't, you can't, never again, and certainly not in front of *her*! I'll call the police, phone your boss, it's outrageous!'

Serge flung off his jacket and chased me into the bathroom. He jammed a foot in the door, and I found myself squatting down and cowering against the side of the bath. He was saying: 'I've got a better idea. You don't even have the decency to shower and dress for a guest, so I'll have to do it for you!'

'You won't!' I shouted. Liliane was at the bathroom door, white-faced, her eyes unnaturally bright.

Serge got my wrap off and handed it to her. He began to instruct her – 'In the bath you'll find a rubber mat. She can show us what she . . .'

'Think again,' I snapped, still hoping that I could escape his grip in view of his drunken state. I knew immediately what he was planning: months ago in the early days, to satisfy one of his quirks, I had used this article to work myself into a frenzy. In those days I would have done anything for him, but now, only a few hours earlier, I had staged a once-and-for-all revolt and had no intention of repeating the performance in front of a stranger.

Everything became clear in an instant. Liliane was his mistress and she was being offered the spectacle of her defeated rival plumbing the depths of degradation! No doubt they had been seeing each other for ages, so no wonder Serge had refused outright that morning to bury the hatchet. It was the obvious explanation, the only possible one I could see at the time.

He eyed my knickers, and I hung on to them firmly. My own eyes flashed to a jumble of jars and bottles next to the bath and, in that split second, he got me in an arm-lock, bent me over and pulled the knickers down. I shouted and kicked and scratched like a tigress. In a final effort I jabbed an elbow at his privates, but I was no match for him.

Liliane now came into the act. On Serge's instructions she placed the rubber mat lengthwise along the edge of the bath and coated it with one of my creams. She then returned to her post in the doorway, and Serge made me straddle the edge of the bath.

'Get going,' he ordered me.

'You'll pay for this, Brossard! I'll take you to court this time, I've nothing to lose now!' I began yelling with all my might so that the neighbours would hear, but he soon stopped that, clamping a towel across my mouth.

He got me horizontal and face down on the mat, my legs dangling either side of the bath. He smacked me mercilessly on my bottom several times, and then removed his belt, swishing it about. I blenched with terror.

'Now start,' he commanded.

'I won't!'

The belt lashed into me and I shrieked. Shaking like a jellyfish I began sliding gingerly back and forth on the slippery surface. It had tiny bumps all over it and these chafed my quim. I began sobbing because I knew I had lost out.

'She loves this,' Serge commented. 'You'll see, she can't resist making an exhibition of herself. Come on, you tramp, lean over, make it rub.'

Liliane said in a soppy voice: 'It's so depraved, I never would have believed it.'

Serge explained: 'It makes a wonderful sex machine, guaranteed to bring her off, it's mechanical.'

I stopped moving and put my tongue out at him, but he menaced me again with the belt.

My tortured crotch was hot from the friction. The rubbery mat made slushy noises, and the effect could not be ignored. As on the previous occasion, every nerve end was roused as the tiny knobs worried my nymphae and clitoris. The entire zone between knees and navel was getting raw. And then the movement gradually hurt less and less and I felt randy.

'You see,' Serge was saying, 'it never fails, she can't stop now. Watch how she flings her head about, the dirty little cat!' he ran his fingers up from my wildly undulating bottom to the nape of my neck. The pleasure increased and I had to stop rocking, clenching my monstrous steed and shuddering fitfully. Suddenly it was as if someone had set a match to my womb and I shook all over, alternately clamping the rubber mat between my thighs then letting my legs fly free as the sensation ransacked my body and I squashed down on my *entrejambe*. Serge squirmed a finger into my rear crack and I roared as a devastating orgasm convulsed me. He had to hold on fast to prevent me toppling sideways.

The pair of them stood watching me gulp in air and jerking to the final spasms. Serge's trouser front had a big bulge in it, Liliane was shifting from one leg to the other, her lips parted.

'Now it's your turn,' I managed to croak.

But Serge led her away. Dismounting carefully, I got into the bath and showered with cool water. I then cleaned everything up, and slowly drew on my knickers and the wrap. All that remained was for me to rinse my face, apply some lipstick and do something with my hair. This took a few minutes, and then I walked into the living room to join my tormentors. The outlines of a plan were forming in my mind.

They were not there, the lounge was empty!

I frowned, then rushed into the bedroom, throwing the door wide. There was Serge lying full-length on Liliane, whose legs were round his middle. They were in the final stages of copulation!

I opened my mouth to speak, and the next thing I knew Serge was bringing me round with little slaps on my cheeks.

Liliane held out a glass of water and I drank it. Nausea returned and I had to lie still for a moment.

We ate the meal in silence except for the odd, meaningless remark. Although I had passed out, I had made my decision the moment I saw my husband and Liliane sullying our marriage bed. I had been blind and utterly gullible, but before the evening was out she would regret she ever set foot in the place. I kept my wrap on for the meal, and Serge did not bother to complain.

So, I reflected as I toyed with the fish, they had been at it for quite a time, and it could reasonably be supposed that the widow would now usurp my place. It was all over between Serge and me. His intention, I supposed, was to hold onto me as his wife in chains until such time, months hence, as he made up his mind to live permanently with Liliane. He might even marry her. One thing was certain, I needed advice, but that could wait until tomorrow.

Throughout the meal I played Serge's game, pretending that I was completely defeated, that I was accepting the arrangement.

The time came to bring in the *île flottante*. This delectable dessert contains the following: white of egg, sugar, vanilla sauce and praline nuts. The end result is featherweight, wobbly and very wet, even if you make it any old how, which I had certainly done that evening. I had told them the dessert was a surprise, and so it turned out to be.

What they were discussing while I fetched it is immaterial, something about Liliane's house. They were facing each other at the oval table and normally I would have resumed my seat between them, serving the dessert from its shallow china dish. But in the event I went behind Liliane, maliciously eying her piled-up copper hair.

'Ah,' said the master of the house, '*Ile flottante*. Laure-Anne does this very well.'

The dish was now poised directly above the lady's coiffure, and I turned it over slowly so that the whole sticky concoction flopped down on her head and ran into her ears, over her face, over her dress and onto her lap.

She jumped up but speech had deserted her. Eventually she released half a dozen squawks. Then she came to life and grabbed my hair, scooped up some of the mess throwing it wide of my head. We locked in battle, aiming to gouge each other's eyes out, we pulled each other's hair, tore our clothes and punched each other's breasts. I thumped and clawed until she lost her balance and hit the sideboard, collapsing onto the floor. At this point Serge rounded the table and weighed into me with slaps to the face. Giggling hysterically I managed to grab the empty dish, and brought it down on his cranium. '*Bonzai!*' I yelled and the two halves of the dish clattered onto the carpet. He exclaimed '*bordel de bordel!*' and sunk to the floor.

Liliane came to and wailed: 'You've murdered him!'

'Not yet!' I shouted. 'And don't you dare come a step nearer or I'll . . . I'll . . .'

The doorbell rang about six times. Dripping with vanilla sauce, half naked now with my breasts wobbling, I wrenched the door open. It was Diane.

'Oh no, not you!' I cried, and slammed the door in her face.

Within seconds I had wiped myself off and was pulling on a fur coat. I ran down the stairs, not knowing or caring whether Serge recovered or died of his injuries. I was incapable of mercy, I wanted him out of the flat dead or alive. Meanwhile I could not bear his very presence.

Chapter Fifteen

After wandering aimlessly about I returned to the flat some time after 1 a.m.. All was deathly quiet.

The night was warm, but the damp air had forced me back home. Wearing only a pair of loose satin knickers under my fur coat, I was shivering when I looked up from the pavement at our windows.

The living room lights were still ablaze. Were the two of them still there or had they cleared off without extinguishing the lights? Or was the homicide squad up there taking pictures of the corpse? There were no parked police cars or ambulances. Once again I had to wake the caretaker, half expecting him to mutter, 'There was a gentleman here asking for you' and so on. I apologised for disturbing him and he lent me the spare set of keys.

Inside the apartment nothing had changed, everything was as I remembered it: the kitchen crammed with bones and scraps and dirty plates, the bedroom in the identical mess that Serge and Liliane had left it in, the living room table covered in food, blobs of *île flottante* seeping into the carpet and the smashed dish lying under a chair. Liliane had lost a single navy blue earring, I noticed, and this was being chivvied about by Cucu who evidently thought it was a cockroach.

'So this is freedom,' I mused, slipping into a warm jogging suit, the one I used on the exercise bike. I turned on *France-Inter* and listened with the all-night drivers and insomniacs. I poured myself the rest of the Vosne-Romanée '74; nothing was too good for *ma rivale*, but it was I who had the last 25 centilitres.

An hour before dawn, and the place was more or less shipshape. I sank onto the settee, too weary to remove the soiled sheets from the bed. They could be consigned to the dustbin later.

On my feet again later that morning, I plugged the phone back in and made coffee.

Cucu purred away happily on my lap as I opened the post for the first time in weeks. My thoughts turned to my family. We were strangers these days. Owing to my profligate and independent way of carrying on over the years, they had disowned me for all practical purposes. I, too, had kept my distance, being unwilling to explain or justify my choice of profession as a club hostess and, later, a club owner. Now that my marriage had ended in disaster I was not going to play the prodigal daughter.

Reflecting soberly in terms of 'I' instead of 'we', I shed no tears. I was still only 30, because I was proud and tough underneath I would pull through somehow. Yes, I would start again. As for Serge, the devil take him. It was a sure bet he would be on the phone or inserting his latchkey later that day, curious to know what I was up to.

I was sad for both of us. I had lost him for reasons I might never understand. The notion that he had genuinely suffered as the outraged husband after the yacht incident and later the trip to Teheran, and had gone along with Liliane to spite me, was absurd. The true explanation must be more complex, and frankly I had no heart to chew it over for the next five decades. Possibly he hated his lady boss and was taking it out on me. It might be that he had always been mentally deranged and I had failed to notice it; perhaps he planned to be Emperor of Europe and had forgotten to mention it.

A clue of a sort turned up when I went through his

pockets and found some white powder. It was crystalline but had no smell. Jumping to conclusions, I put some on the tip of my tongue and it went numb for a while. My conclusions were correct, the substance was certainly cocaine, and he had been using it on himself and no doubt on Liliane. I knew enough about police procedure to suppose that evidence found during a drug swoop went into plastic bags and not into loose pockets. It was reasonable to suppose he had simply taken some pickings for himself.

I routed out Jacquot's phone number at the depot. Yes, he was in France but taking some days holiday that were due to him. He was expected to drop in the next morning, no I couldn't have his home number but they would give him mine.

There was no mistaking his craggy voice when he came on the line: 'Is that Madame Brossard?' He said he had been nowhere special, just to Teheran twice, then to Le Havre and back several times.

'What's the trouble?' he asked quickly.

'No trouble,' I said lightheartedly. 'At least I don't think so. My husband and I have split up, but I'm not sure what's likely to happen now. Anyhow I'm sorry I'm costing you more money with this call. Are you at home? Give me your number and I'll phone back. Nobody's paying our phone bill at the moment.' He refused to ring off, but I extracted his home number from him.

I said: 'Listen Jacquot, I simply want to say that I haven't forgotten what I owe you, and if you send me your address . . .'

'*Tu blagues*. I'd like to see you again.'

'Me too, love to.'

There was an awkward pause, then he said: 'You mean your bloke has cleared off, or is it the other way round?'

'It's too early to say, but I'm in possession at the moment. I'll call again soon. I mean it Jacquot, I grew to like you a lot on that trip.'

'Me, too.'

'Well, that's great.' We were like Meryl Streep and Robert De Niro in the film *Falling in Love*!

'We could take it further perhaps,' he said.

'Sure thing. Say Jacquot, I'm glad you called back, you can't imagine how much it's cheered me up.'

'I'll call again, let me do the calling. Well, *ciao* for now.'

'*Ciao*.'

My eyes were smarting when I replaced the receiver. He seemed to be the only friend I had in the world.

Our banal but refreshing exchange of courtesies made it infinitely easier for me to remain self-possessed when Serge rang.

'*Bonjour, c'est moi*.' he said.

'*Bonjour*.' A long pause. 'It's your turn now.'

'My turn?'

'To say *bonjour*, or anything else that springs to mind.'

'I thought you may have left, gone home to your family.'

'I have no family. This is my home.'

'Anything in the mail?'

'No, there hasn't been for days. I've no doubt you are having it redirected to the office.'

'How clever of you to work it out.'

'Like I told you, I have brains as well, but you never noticed.' Another pause and I waited.

'You're very quiet.'

'I'm too weak to talk, I don't eat much. No money, no food, no strength. Logical.'

'We ought to meet.'

'No car either. No money for the bus fare.'

'Hm.'

'How's your lady friend? Has she recovered?'

'She's recovered.'

He came round, and had the decency to ring the bell rather than let himself in. He brought a suitcase and looked the picture of misery. As far as I was concerned the widow was welcome to him.

'Symbolic, the suitcase,' I said. 'So you're moving out. Thanks for the furniture.'

'You haven't got it yet, or even the apartment.'

'Nor have you, you need my signature. Well have a drink – while it lasts.'

He put the suitcase down in the hall and we sat in the lounge clutching our drinks as if we had never tasted anything stronger than orange juice.

I said, 'I won't grovel this time, so don't be afraid. I'm curious to know what she's got that I haven't, apart from a nice house and an expensive hairdresser.' He shrugged and I added: 'She's your problem now. What do you have in mind for me?'

'I'm still thinking it out.'

'Talking it out with her? I suppose you want a divorce.'

'And you?'

'I asked the question first.'

'I'm thinking it out, don't rush me.'

'I have to. I possess exactly 476 francs to live on. In 24 hours I apply to the court. You have abandoned the domicile.'

'Prove it. I'll phone next week when I've had time to think what's best.'

'You think too slowly. It won't look good, proof or no proof, when I go to the court tomorrow. Now take what you want and clear out.'

'I may come back. I'll phone tomorrow, midday or evening.'

'Make it midday. I'm going to the court at 3 p.m.'

At midday, however, I was in a bistro with Blandine.

'When the electric razor goes out through the door, it's the beginning of the end,' she affirmed. 'It means he's not buying another one, he's gone for good.'

'I suppose you're right.'

'Forget him, find a lawyer quick.'

She took a swig from her double gin and Martini. My Ricard stood untouched. I took her hand, reflecting not for the first time that friendship is deeper and lasts longer than what people are pleased to call love. I was too bitter at present to give love a chance.

'Thanks for coming,' I said with a catch in my voice.

'I wish I could be of some use. Of course, in practice it'll be a battle of wills, it usually is, but you must simply hold out.'

The hot sun shone brightly through the big window. The bar was busy at this hour and a thick layer of tobacco smoke swirled in the sunlight beneath the ceiling.

I told Blandine: 'My problem at the moment is, who pays the bills? They could cut off the phone and electricity.'

'Let the bills pile up. Get a lawyer's letter off to him. How much have you got anyway?'

'I have 393 francs in my purse, and that's the lot.'

Blandine's jaw dropped: 'He's starving you into submission?'

'I'll find work. I can get unemployment pay.'

'I doubt if you'll get dole money. You could come back to Les Chabannes for a while, only to work though – you mustn't leave the flat empty.' She shook her fists above the table at an imaginary Serge Brossard: '*Le salaud, quelle ordure!* I hope you hit him hard with that dish.'

I swallowed most of my Ricard in one go: 'Hard enough. You're very kind, Blandine my sweet, but I couldn't join you. It comes down to something very simple – I've had about as much sex as I can stand, I can't even bear a love scene on TV. If anyone as much as approached me in my present mood I'd disfigure them for life. It'll take time, it'll take quite a time.'

Blandine ordered more drinks: 'The legal wrangle could take months, although a good lawyer can arrange payments. Look, Laure-Anne, I'm stacking up reserves, living on Les Chabannes and my investments. I'd be more than glad to advance you a loan, interest-free naturally. It's the least I can do, that's what friends are for. No, I insist. Get it into your pretty head that I don't need the money. I impose only one condition, that you immediately start looking for work. It'll give you an interest, apart from anything else.'

'I haven't worked for 18 months. If any money is coming my way I might start up my own business.'

'I'll give you a week to produce a four-page report. That's an order.'

We laughed and kicked the business ideas back and forth. Blandine wrote out a sizeable cheque.

'I won't cash it,' I said.

'You will, or I'll deliver the money personally in an armoured van.'

Four rings and I lifted the receiver.

'I've been calling all afternoon. You weren't in at midday.'

'I had an urgent appointment.'

'Did you make enquiries?'

'Yes,' I lied.

'And?'

'They're looking into it.'

'Well you can call off the dogs. Rather than support you for the rest of your life, I've fixed up for the divorce. As there are no children involved it should go through automatically. It will probably take about three months.'

'What are you driving at?'

'We split half and half, meaning the apartment and what's in it, and the bank. Plus compensation, that means in practice the other half of the apartment for you. You'll own the flat and have some money too.'

'That's fair. It was virtually all my money to begin with. You'll come out of it well, too, she's a good catch financially. Are you going to marry her?'

'I'll have to think carefully about that.'

'Think away, *mon vieux*. It's sad, you know, I thought we would do great things together. Well, see you in court.'

'That's about it.'

Seconds later I was on the wire to Jacquot.

'Any chance of you calling in?'

'You just gave me the chance. After all we're not like snails, they make love only twice a year.'

'How sad.'

151

'Yes, but when they do it lasts for eight hours. Ha-ha-ha.'

'How nice. Jacquot, *mon chou*, have you a lot of stories like that? I adore the way you tell them.'

'A whole camel train, on beauteous memsahib.'

'Would you like to leave Valenciennes for good and tell your stories to the customers over the bar?'

'What customers?'

'Yours and mine. I have a proposition for you. How much money can you lay your hands on in three or four months' time?'

He thought for a while: 'At a rough guess I'd say about 400,000, plus any loans I can get.'

'We're in business. My stake's ready.'

'But w-where . . . ?'

'Don't know yet. Somewhere between Marseille and the Italian border. When can we discuss it?'

'Give me five minutes to saddle up and I'm on my way. See you around midnight. Sounds like a terrific idea of yours. We could hire a piano player and a girl singer and everything . . .'

I gave him directions and told him: 'You won't let me down, Jacquot? You *will come*?'

'You can count on me!'

My voice had a wistful note to it: 'I know I can, Jacquot, I know it.'